GUNNER

BROTHERS COURAGEOUS

VANESSA GRAY BARTAL

DRY CREEK PRESS

PROLOGUE

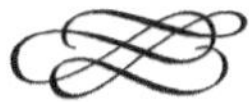

*A*shton Rucker shouldered his bag and walked away without a backward glance. Did anyone look back? Did anyone think, "Parris Island, I'm going to miss that place. Gee, boot camp was great!" No. Everyone hated it. But as much as he had loathed it, he had also somehow enjoyed it. Maybe he hadn't enjoyed the process, but he was happy with the final effect. For the first time in his eighteen years, he felt capable. Capable enough to handle whatever life threw at him, namely his mother.

For as long as he could remember, Ashton had been taking care of her as best he could, but it had never been good enough. Now that was all about to change because he finally realized the problem wasn't him; it was his mother. He couldn't give her the help she needed, but he could make sure and find someone who could. He had ten days before he had to report to School of Infantry. Ten days to deal with his mother and her depression once and for all. Before leaving basic, he had swallowed his pride and contacted a base psychologist to ask her advice. For the first time, Ashton was armed with a handful of pamphlets for inpatient facilities that could give his mother a handle on her mental illness. The trick would be convincing her to go, but he wouldn't take no for an answer. He would carry her there if he had to.

Leaving for basic had been the hardest thing he had ever done. Staying away for thirteen weeks, leaving his mother on her own, had nearly killed him. He had done it for himself, but he had done it for her, too. Or so he told himself. With a career, he would be able to support her much better than by continuing to work at the oil-changing place for minimum wage. There was a little part of him, the little part he wasn't willing to acknowledge, that had been relieved to go. And that part made him feel unbelievably guilty. But it had also given him the strength and determination to succeed. There had only been a few times when he'd had the passing temptation to give up, but then he had remembered what was waiting for him at home. And he had kept going. The marines were not only a way out of his situation, they were a chance to change it.

He was luckier than most who were leaving basic because his hometown was in South Carolina, a short bus ride from the base. Four hours after he left Parris Island, he was home, such as it was. Trash filtered out of his mother's small rental house, filling up the porch and spilling into the yard. When he lived at home, his bedroom had been the one place untouched by her hoarding. That probably wasn't the case anymore. He would no doubt have to spend hours clearing it out, listening to his mother tell him not to throw away any of her priceless treasures. She lived under the constant delusion that either someone would come along and recognize something valuable among the junk and offer her a lot of money or that someday something she had saved would come in handy for a particular situation. Need an umbrella? Good thing because she has fifty of them. Of course they're all broken, but try telling her that.

Before he could ascend the walkway and pick his way around the trash piles, the neighbor's door banged open and a man rushed out.

"We can't have this anymore," Mr. Willard yelled, indicating the trash with a wave of his hand. "I've called the city and they've assured me it's a clear violation of code. They're going to take action. I know your mama has some, er, *arrangement* with her landlord, but it doesn't matter anymore. She's got to clear this up or go. My vote is for her to go."

It was at that moment Ashton realized how much basic training had changed him. Any previous mention of his mother's arrangement with the landlord—meaning she gave him personal favors in exchange for the house—would have shamed him to silence. But he had realized his mother's mistakes weren't his. Her shame was her own. And even though the man was making him murderously angry with his threats and accusations, Ashton wouldn't retaliate. He would simply show him the respect due a stranger.

"I'm hoping to get things cleared up in the next week, sir. I apologize for the mess," he said.

"See that you do," the old man said, pointing a stubby finger in Ashton's face. "Because I'm sick and tired of living next door to this trash, and I'm not talking about the stuff on the lawn."

Ashton had to take a breath at that one, to remind himself this man wasn't worth losing his new career over. "My mother is ill, and you'll do well not to speak of her that way again."

The man blinked at him, withdrawing his finger and tucking it in his pocket. "Well, see that it gets cleared up," he added, much more subdued and quiet now. With renewed meekness, he turned and walked back to his house.

Despite the trash, the ugly confrontation, and the pending ordeal of seeing his mother, Ashton felt good. He had handled the situation differently than before. Usually whenever someone talked about his mother—as the whole town was apt to do—he had either retreated into shameful silence or lashed out in uncontrollable rage. Handling himself like a mature adult was a much better approach, and one he would use from now on.

"Mama, I'm home." His attempt to push open the door fell short because there was so much trash in the way. Using his boot, he shimmied and pushed until he opened it enough to walk inside. Maybe while his mother was in the mental hospital, he would use some of the new money from his job and have the house cleaned out. She would be livid when she learned he threw away the junk, but maybe it would give her a fresh start.

"Mama," he called. There was so much trash in the room it swallowed the sound of his voice. "Mama," he tried again, louder this time, but it still didn't carry down the hall. He would have to walk inside eventually; it might as well be now.

Hefting his bag higher so it didn't get caught, he began slowly walking down the hall, at times stepping over piles of trash as tall as his waist. The many piles bore testament to how much his mother had suffered during his absence. They had never been this many or this high before.

He was so intent on not falling that it took him a while to notice the unnatural silence of the house. Was his mother sleeping? He knew she was home because, in addition to her many other fears, she was also agoraphobic, preferring to never leave the house. She even had her groceries delivered, though Ashton didn't like to think about that because it was another man who brought them, another man who received special favors as payment.

What if she had fallen and was buried somewhere under the rubble? He might never find her. By the time he reached her bedroom and pushed open the door, he was almost panicked, but she wasn't there. No longer caring if his bag got dirty, he tossed it aside and began digging through the piles of rotting garbage on her floor, sure that she must be stuck there somewhere. He was sweating by the time he was finished, but he still didn't find her.

He walked through all the rooms of the house with no success, all the rooms but one. The door to his bedroom was closed. His heart hammered as he made his way back down the hall. Somehow he knew whatever he was going to find wasn't going to be good, but nothing could have prepared him for what he found when he opened the door.

There was no trash. The room was as immaculate as the day he left. But there was also his mother, her lifeless form swinging from a rope in the middle of the ceiling.

CHAPTER 1

Shelby Lance was doing it; she was succeeding. As the lone failure in a family of overachievers, the feeling was new to her. Now that she had experienced a taste of doing well, she was hooked. Things would be different when she returned to the states. No longer would she be Shelby-the-loser. She would be Shelby-with-a-purpose, someone to make her parents proud.

This is our daughter, Shelby. She spent a few months as an aid worker in Saudi Arabia. This is our daughter, Shelby. She works hard to change the world. Maybe that was a little over-the-top. She couldn't imagine her parents ever saying such a thing, but at least they would have something to add to her name instead of the usual *This is Shelby,* followed by a heavy silence. She had always been such a contrast to her older siblings.

"This is Marcus, he's getting his doctorate. This is Jennifer, she's earning her MD. This is Alicia, she's finishing her master's. And this is Shelby." That was the way the introductions went in her family. Usually Shelby would be standing somewhere nearby because she was also the only one who still lived at home. So she had to hold her breath and wait to see if the person she was being presented to would merely stare at her in curiosity or actually be nosy enough to add the ubiquitous, "And what do you do, Shelby?"

She never had a good answer to that question before. Now she did. "I'm an aid worker. I travel the world. I just got back from Saudi Arabia." Except she wasn't back yet, she was still in Saudi Arabia, walking the streets on market day, her hijab swathing her head and making her sweat. She had dreaded wearing the thing, though she wasn't stupid enough to try and argue with millennia of rules dictating its use. But then she arrived and her aunt presented her with one she had commissioned for her. Shelby wasn't a seamstress, but even she could recognize the talent and work that went into the intricate trim. Now as she walked, she often looked at the hijabs the other women wore, wondering what they signified. Had a husband bought it? A mother? Had the woman noticed it and decided she had to have it? She began to understand that a hijab could be both a sign of submission and a statement of independence as each woman wore one tailored to suit her own tastes and personality.

Shelby had never thought of herself as being sheltered before, but being here made her understand how little she knew about the world. Growing up half Saudi and half American should have given her a greater cultural awareness, but her mother had shirked the vestiges of her homeland for her adopted country, leaving Shelby as clueless about the Middle East as any other American. She had learned so much already, not merely about the culture, the country, and her family, but about herself. She couldn't wait to go home and apply all the new knowledge and information.

"Hello, Cousin." Amalfi sidled up beside her, touching his fingers to her elbow. Besides being her cousin, he was her closest friend in the country. Shelby was happy to leave it at that, but Amalfi's interest went deeper—a cultural difference Shelby did not embrace. She had no interest in dating or marrying her cousin, even though the practice was common here. His unabashed attraction to her gave her the creeps, but she constantly reminded herself she was the outsider with the strange ideas here. Amalfi was doing what came naturally.

"Hello, Malfy," Shelby said. Her family was kind enough to speak

English for her. Arabic was something else she should have picked up from her mother, but she had naively believed Saudi Arabians would accommodate her lack of language skills—a notion that now seemed smug, especially because she never had any idea what anyone was saying. Even her cousins sometimes spoke with such a strong accent that she had trouble understanding them. There was no misunderstanding Amalfi today, however. He had the look, the one that meant he was once more going to try and take their relationship somewhere she definitely didn't want it to go.

"I thought perhaps I may walk with you, and then we could have dinner this evening," Amalfi suggested.

"What is Aunt making for supper?" Shelby asked, feigning innocence.

Amalfi looked away, baffled at how to proceed. As Shelby's departure date grew closer, her cousin grew bolder in his attempts to entice her. It was her secret thought that he hoped they would marry and provide him a free pass to the United States. He was fascinated with her country and spent a lot of time talking about Eminem—someone Shelby knew little to nothing about.

"I thought perhaps we could have a meal alone," Amalfi said.

Shelby stifled a sigh. He was sweet, guileless, and even handsome. But he was her *cousin*. How did she possibly make him understand that, being American, she found his attention repulsive? "That's very nice, Malfi, but I have so little time left here. I would love to spend the evening with all our family." *Your aunt—my mother's sister. Ew.*

"Oh, I see." His expressive obsidian eyes were wounded, and Shelby felt terrible.

"Malfi, I like you, I really do. You're a very good friend to me."

"In America, this is what's called a brushoff, is it not?" he asked.

"It's that we're cousins. I know things are different here, but I can't think of you as anything more than my cousin. I'm sorry." She bit her lip, waiting for his reaction. She didn't want to offend or hurt him.

His smile was wry. "Isn't it ironic that my only possible route to America is closed off because of your American ideals?"

"It's not closed. Come for a visit. I'll introduce you to some of my friends. Maybe you'll fall instantly in love, get married, and stay forever."

He laughed. "I like the way you think, Cousin Shelby. I'll see you at home."

He was smiling as he walked away, giving Shelby the hope that no permanent damage had been done by her rebuff. She felt sunny and cheerful as she strolled through the market. Merchants shouted at her, announcing their wares. She had no idea what they were saying, but they seemed to instinctively know she was American because they were trying extra hard to earn her attention and money. She was in such a good mood that she didn't at first notice the men behind her. When she did, she felt immediate alarm. There was something in their eyes, something far removed from the warmth and friendliness of her male relatives.

Shelby picked up her pace, attempting to outmaneuver them. Whenever she glanced behind, however, they were there, hedging closer and closer until she began to run. Panic claimed her, leading her away from the market and into a remote area of the city until at last she reached a dead end.

She stopped and spun, praying the men wouldn't be there, but they were. She forced her hands to her sides, her fingers curled into fists in what she hoped was a strong, defensive pose. "I have only a small amount of money, but you can have it," she said. Her traitorous voice trembled, making a show of her defiance.

They said something in Arabic, inching closer as they herded her into a corner. She had no idea what they said, but their tone was clearly menacing. Her back bumped the wall and she whimpered. "Please," she begged, not attempting to be brave anymore. "Please don't hurt me." One reached up to touch her face and she winced, turning her head to the side. He roughly jerked her toward him again as he made his inspection.

His breath was hot on her face, and it smelled of onions and garlic. Shelby squeezed her eyes closed and then opened them when a bag was shoved roughly over her head. It was dark, hot, and uncomfortable. She was immediately claustrophobic and began to reach for the bag, intending to rip it off her head. Strong arms subdued her, a needle jabbed her arm, and everything faded away.

Sometime later she woke, the bag still over her head. What had they given her? She ached all over. Where was she? What day was it? She was afraid to call out, to draw attention to the fact that she was awake, and yet she had to know where she was. Maybe they had let her go

"Hello," she tried, her voice small and timid.

Another voice answered in Arabic. It was vaguely familiar and she recognized it as belonging to one of the men who had kidnapped her. The hood was jerked roughly off her face. She blinked, squinting against the sudden rush of light. Her throat was tight and parched; she longed for water almost as much as she longed for freedom.

"Where am I?" she tried, but the men standing before her didn't answer. There were five of them, all staring at her with an expression she didn't understand. At least she didn't understand until the door opened and the men turned to look. The feeling of expectancy increased as the sixth man walked into the room. Shelby could tell he was the leader of whoever they were.

"Please, may I have some water?" she tried. The leader walked slowly across the room and came to a stop in front of her. Then he lifted his hand and struck her so hard across the face her head tipped to the side. She cried out in pain and fear, and the bag was roughly shoved back onto her head. *Please let that be it,* she prayed. *Please let them leave now.* But her prayer was not to be answered. Strong arms jerked her from the chair and flung her onto the floor. One man held her down while another pulled up her robe. Shelby gave up trying to be quiet or calm then. She screamed and flailed, attempting to get away, but to no avail. The iron arms were too strong, and the group of men oblivious to her pleas.

CHAPTER 2

"Melly wouldn't even say goodbye to me. Did you know?"

"Yes, I know because you told me on the plane over the ocean. And then when we landed in Turkey. Then on the chopper to the drop zone. And twice since we've been in this hole," Nick said. He should probably be doing sit ups or push-ups or something other than sitting here listening to Kelsey rehash his misery for the tenth time, but he was tired, and they were rationing their food and water. Conserving energy was important. Or so he told himself.

"Oh, so sorry Mr. I'm-in-love-and-can't-listen-to-anyone's-problems."

"Fine. Tell me again. Melly wouldn't say goodbye to you."

"Yeah. I go over to her place to, you know, make amends like we usually do before I go wheels up, and she won't speak to me. And I'm like, 'Melly, what the crud, I'm going overseas and you're not even going to say goodbye? What if I don't come back?' And you know what she says?"

"Yes, but tell me again," Nick said.

"She says, 'You're not going to die, Kelsey, because only the good die young, but you'd better take care of my baby brother and bring him back safe. Now get out of my house.'"

"And then she shoved you out the door and slammed it in your face," Nick finished.

"Wait, have you heard this before?" Kelsey said.

"We've all heard it," Truck said. "We have it memorized by now, you pathetic loser." It was his turn on watch, so he didn't take his eye off the scope.

"Why's she so mad at you this time?" Nick asked.

"I don't know. She's all hopped up on female hormones. Who can explain women?" Kelsey said.

Truck kicked an empty food container toward his head. "She's mad at you because you borrowed her car to troll for women, left it in the parking lot too long, and then made her pay the tow recovery fee."

"Hey, I'm good for it. She knows that," Kelsey said.

"She's knows you're a pathetic loser," Truck reiterated.

"Truck's right, Jaws" Lolly said. He was lying on the floor, attempting to sleep and probably irritated that Kelsey's story was keeping him awake. "Why don't you admit you love her and get it over with?"

"What? I mean, okay, I love her, but like a sister," Kelsey said.

"No, *I* love her like a sister," Lolly said. "You love her like Whit loves Ashleigh."

"Pathetically?" Kelsey said, dodging Nick's blow when he gave a half-hearted lunge.

"Yes," Truck said. "Exactly. You guys are enough to make me lose my lunch."

"Hey, don't lump me in with him. I got my woman, and we're getting married. I'm not a loser anymore," Nick said.

"Yeah," Kelsey said, then frowned. "Hey, wait, that wasn't the resounding defense I expected."

"That's because it wasn't a defense. Lolly's right; Marry Melly and have lots of babies," Nick said.

"Just because you've gone all soft over a woman doesn't mean the rest of us have to. Melly and I are friends. When we're not trying to kill each other."

"Whatever," Nick and Lolly said together.

"There's actually something I wanted to talk to you guys about," Nick said.

Kelsey leaned back against the wall with a thump. "Uh-oh. Must be bad."

"Why?" Nick said.

"Because we've been stuck in this house for forty eight hours, forty eight mind-numbing hours, one of which we spent speculating over how much lint is actually contained in the belly button of the average male, and you didn't mention whatever it is you're about to mention. That means you've been working up to it. That means it's bad," Kelsey said. Lolly sat up and moved closer. Truck didn't move, but his hand tensed on the scope.

"It's not bad. At least, I don't think it is. I've been accepted to Officer Candidate School at Quantico. I'm leaving when we get back."

"Congratulations, man," Lolly exclaimed. He reached over and thumped Nick on the leg. "In what universe would that be bad news?"

Kelsey knew, however. "Because it probably means the end of our team."

The room became silent then. "Won't they put us back together when Nick is done with OCS?" Lolly asked.

"You really think they're going to put our team on hold indefinitely while Nick's at school? No, they're going to assign us another shooter or break us up entirely," Truck said.

Kelsey was quiet for a while, but then he piped up, too. "Congratulations, man, really. We knew this day was coming, and we're all happy for you, even if it seems like we're only thinking of ourselves. Ashleigh's going to freak when you tell her."

"I already told her," Nick said.

"You told her before us?" Kelsey said.

"She's going to be my wife. She sort of needed to know," Nick said.

"But we're your brothers. Since when does wife trump brothers?" Kelsey asked.

"Since man figure out that he could create another human being with wife," Nick said. "I love you guys, you know that, but what

Ashleigh and I have sort of outweighs what we have going. Sorry if that's harsh, but someday you'll fall in love and you'll understand."

"Or we won't," Truck said. "Did it ever occur to you not everyone wants to be in love?"

"I used to think that," Nick said. "Until it happened to me."

"I threw up in my mouth a little," Kelsey declared.

"Wait and see," Nick said, sounding old and sage even though he, Kelsey, and Ashton were the same age.

"We've got movement," Truck said, and all the levity was sucked from the room as Kelsey and Nick rushed toward the window. Truck rolled away as he tossed the scope to Kelsey.

"Is it our guy?" Nick said. He assumed the position by picking up his weapon and settling it into the groove he had formed on arrival. The shot wasn't perfect, but the weapon couldn't be exposed. He had to take a slight angle, but it was better than risking a flash of sunlight gleaming off the stock. Of course that wasn't a problem now because it was almost night and the sun was on the other side of the building.

"C'mon, c'mon, move," Kelsey muttered. "There's a crowd."

"I see," Nick said, looking through the scope on his gun now.

"There's a woman," Kelsey exclaimed. "I thought this guy's wife was in Jordan."

"That's what our intel said," Nick replied.

"Intel," Truck said. "As if they've never gotten anything wrong before." In the field, they often had to rely on whatever information the CIA could cull for them. They much preferred the missions where they did their own recon, but sometimes, like now, that wasn't possible. They had been staked out in their hiding spot for two days with no chance to leave for fear of missing their target, which made them all tense because it felt like they were going into a situation blind.

"It's him," Kelsey said. "It's definitely him."

Nick didn't have a clear enough view to see details of the guy's face, but, unlike the CIA, he trusted Kelsey. If Kelsey said it was him, then it was him. The problem was the woman. Who was she and what was she doing there? Their information hadn't said anything about a woman. Should he take the shot or wait for a time when the man was alone?

"Are you taking it or not?" Kelsey asked.

Nick was used to making split decisions in the field, but that never meant it was easy. He had a clear headshot now. If he waited, he might not have the opportunity again. "I'm taking it," he said. "What's my range?" He knew because he had done his own calculations, but he and Kelsey had their own little system and routine, so he asked the question he always asked before he took the shot.

"900. Winds west southwest," Kelsey said. He kept his scope pressed to his eye, waiting and watching.

Nick took a breath, making sure in that split second that he was properly aligned and still out of sight, and then he squeezed the trigger. Kelsey watched his vapor trail in case he missed and needed to recalculate, but Nick watched the target, his gut clenching with mixed emotions when the man's head exploded into mist. The woman was standing so close that she must be covered with his blood and brain matter. Whoever she was, Nick hoped she would somehow recover from the trauma, but that was as far as he went in personalizing the moment. It was better for him to remain aloof, to think of the person he had just killed as the nameless, faceless bad guy, even though he had memorized his name and face three days ago while being briefed in the US.

Kelsey swore and Nick turned to look up at him. He had hit the target; what was the problem? "The woman looked up here," he said. "I don't know how, but I think she saw us."

"Did the guards see?" Lolly asked.

"No, but it's only a matter of time until she begins pointing, and then we're stuck here like sitting ducks," Truck said, adding a fluent stream of curse words that made Nick cringe. He had promised himself he would stop cursing if Ashleigh said yes to his proposal, and now he was sensitized to every word he wouldn't allow himself to say.

"Pack it up, let's go," Nick said. He rolled away from the window and stood, already disassembling his gun and loading it in its case.

"Wait," Kelsey said and everyone froze. "She's rabbiting."

"What?" Truck said. He came forward to look, even though he couldn't see anything without the scope.

"She's using the chaos as a chance to run," Kelsey said. "Whoever she is, I don't think she was there by choice."

"She's going to run right for us," Truck said. "She's going to lead them here."

"No," Kelsey replied. "She's going north. So far no one is chasing her." He swore again and leaned farther out the window. "I lost her."

Truck grabbed the back of his shirt and jerked. "They'll see you, moron. Why don't you wave a neon semaphore flag and save yourself some time."

"What do we do?"

Everyone turned to Nick, looking for direction. He paused, his mind quickly running through scenarios. There was a good possibility that the woman still might be heading toward them. She might lead guards in their direction which wouldn't be a catastrophe, but it would put a serious dent in their plan to get in and out with minimal disruption.

On the other hand, their chopper wasn't due to arrive for three more days. They could either wait in the safety of this building, or they could take their chances in the desert where the woman and guards *still* might find them.

"We wait here, but we step up our patrols to include the perimeter," he said. With one of them constantly patrolling the perimeter and another standing by on the scope, there was no way anyone could sneak by and catch them unaware.

"I'm up," Lolly said. He stood and shouldered his weapon, making his way down the rickety stairs for the first four hour shift.

"I'm sleeping," Kelsey said. He tossed the scope to Nick and lay down, falling immediately asleep in the way they had all been trained to do. Sleep was vital, and they took it where and when they could get it.

"Sleep," Nick said to Truck who leaned against the wall, using his gun as a pillow. Nick didn't understand how that was comfortable, but since he had seen Truck do the same thing on more than one occasion, he figured it was more about security than comfort.

Palming the scope, he turned toward the window, looking for any sign of the mystery woman.

CHAPTER 3

"Obviously the woman wasn't his wife," Kelsey said. He was back on post at the window. Truck had just woken up. He and Nick were sharing a meal before Truck went to relieve Lolly and Nick fell asleep.

"Why?" Nick said. "Because she ran away? We know how these men treat their women. Maybe she got tired of being beaten and raped."

"No. You know how it is; the culture is brainwashed. They think it's their duty and they're killed for running away," Kelsey argued. "She was someone else."

"I know who she was," Truck said. Kelsey and Nick looked at him in surprise.

"Who?" Nick said, probably wondering how he got his hands on some intel.

"She was their toy," Truck said. He saw the way the men looked at her before he tossed the scope to Kelsey. It was the same way men used to look at his mother, with a combination of possession and revulsion. She took care of their needs, but they hated her just the same.

"You think she was a prostitute?" Kelsey said. "How could you tell so quickly?"

"I just could," Truck said. They didn't argue with him, not because they knew the particulars of his childhood, but because the level of trust between them was that high, especially in the field. If Truck thought she was a hooker, then they would believe him because he wasn't given to hyperbolic speculation and they knew it.

"Even so, things must have been pretty bad for her to run away," Kelsey said. "I bet they treated her awful."

"It was probably nothing less than what she deserved," Truck said and, that was probably over the line because both Nick and Kelsey turned to look at him in surprise. And it was more than likely that their surprise held a hint of recrimination, too. "I'm just saying, you live that life, it's going to have consequences."

"Maybe that's true in the US," Nick said. "But what choice do these women have? Death or prostitution. It's easy to be on the outside looking in and say death is a more noble choice. But maybe she has kids to think about."

"If she has kids to think about, then she definitely shouldn't be hooking. I don't care where we are. There are always choices," Truck said. There was definitely a lot of bitterness in his tone, and Whit and Jaws definitely noticed. But they didn't call him on it, and that was why he loved them. He could be himself with them, even when who he was was a pretty miserable human being. The two of them plus Lolly were the first examples of unconditional love he had ever encountered in his life, and he returned it wholeheartedly. There was nothing he wouldn't do for any of them, including dying.

He squeezed out the last of his MRE spaghetti, wishing for a cherry-blueberry cobbler. Being from the south, he believed no meal was complete without dessert. But they had packed light for this mission, and even though the packets of cobbler were small, they were still a luxury. His mind drifted to Nick's fiancée, Ashleigh, and her peach cobbler. If there was one thing he envied about their relationship, it was Ashleigh's skills in the kitchen. She often cooked for the team, and it was amazing. What would it be like to have someone to go home to? Someone who loved you and served warm treats from the oven on a daily basis?

He shook his head and stood, tossing the empty MRE containers into the corner they had designated for trash. He was a fool to daydream about something that would never be his. Women wanted too much, needed too much, and Ashton was all tapped out.

He jogged down the stairs to relieve Lolly. "Psst," he called. Lolly jogged over and they exchanged weapons. Ashton's machine gun was good for mowing down anything in their path, but it wasn't exactly subtle. Lolly's gun was subtle and better for surveillance, but being so far in hostile territory, they didn't go anywhere unarmed, not even to the stairwell. Lolly took the machine gun and jogged up the stairs while Ashton stepped out into the inky blackness and pulled his night vision goggles over his face.

Ashton would never admit it to his teammates, but walking sentry was the job he hated the most. It wasn't merely that it was mind-numbingly boring to walk in a circle around the perimeter of a building for four hours. Boredom he could handle. Sitting inside the house was boring, but he didn't mind. But there was something unique about the combination of walking and boredom that caused his thoughts to clear. As always when his mind calmed and opened, his memories came to the surface. Memories of his cruddy childhood and cruddier adolescence. Memories of finding his mother swinging from a rope in his room, of standing on the street a day after her funeral as a crew of garbage men hauled the tons of trash from her house. It had been almost ten years since that awful time. Would the images never go away?

He was nearing the end of his shift when he caught a furtive move-ment in his peripheral vision. He turned slowly, training his weapon on a massive pile of rubble that used to be a home. His finger steadied on the trigger. "Come out," he said, employing one of the Arabic phrases he knew by heart.

It was the woman, the prostitute who ran from the target. She stepped into view, her hands held aloft. Ten scenarios ran through Ashton's mind, and none of them were good. Most of them ended with the fact that this woman had somehow found them, meaning either she was a professional or she'd had help. Which meant this might be a trap. Through his goggles, he could see that her face was filled with fear, but he had learned not to trust the women of this area after his first deployment as a marine. Someone in his unit had made that mistake and paid with his life. He thought of that now, the way he had watched the marine die because of a woman, the way men had trusted and used his mother, the way this woman earned her keep by selling herself, and he was disgusted.

"If you're here to try and whore yourself out to us, you've come to the wrong place," he said. He used English because he knew she wouldn't understand, but then she spoke.

"Please, I need some help." Her English was perfect with no trace of an accent. Her arms dropped to her sides as she wilted to the ground in a dead faint. At least it looked like a faint. Ashton knew better than to rush forward because that was inevitably the moment when her companions rushed from around the building and killed him.

So he remained where he was, his weapon trained on her inert form as he scanned the area, straining to listen for any sounds that didn't belong. After a full moment of utter silence, he slipped forward and crouched beside her, pressing his weapon to the base of her skull with one hand while he began to frisk her with the other. Once again he knew better than to make a mistake with the frisking. There were some marines who freaked out over the thought of frisking a woman, but a woman was prone to hiding a weapon as much as a man, maybe more so because of their voluminous robes. So after he skimmed his hand over the outside of her legs, he began running it up the inside, and that's when he felt it. Removing his weapon so he could lean down for a closer inspection, he withdrew his hand and held it up to the moonlight. Then he shouldered his weapon, scooped the woman into his arms, and carried her up the stairs.

"I've got a bleeder," he announced as he entered the room where his buddies were staying and deposited the woman on the floor. In a practiced movement, he slid the weapon off his shoulder and handed it to Kelsey who didn't pause before turning to jog down the stairs.

The sight of an injured woman was alarming on a number of levels but mostly because it meant she might not be alone. They would need to be even more vigilant about their patrols in case she had been followed. Nick woke and picked up the scope, scanning outside the window, leaving Lolly and Truck to see to the woman's care.

Of all of them, Lolly had the most medical training. Someday when he was out of the marines, he intended to be a paramedic. Medicine was his hobby, and he had taken multiple classes, making him the team's go-to person for medical care. But he was also shy and sensitive, and therefore reluctant to pull up the woman's robe and take a look.

"Do you want me to do it?" Truck asked. He didn't have the medical training, but he also wasn't squeamish. Finding his mother's deceased body after two days in a hot South Carolina house pretty much topped anything else he might see for the rest of his life.

"I'll do it," Lolly said. He closed his eyes, murmured a prayer, lifted the robe, and looked. Then he abruptly turned away, pulled the rosary out of his pocket, and pressed it to his lips.

"What is it?" Truck asked. "Is she dying? Did they gut her?"

Lolly shook his head. "They…they brutalized her. She's bleeding from the…they must have raped her. A lot."

Truck swore. Lolly put his head between his knees and sucked oxygen. He was tenderhearted when it came to women, something his other teammates had tried to warn him about, but to no avail.

"Lolly, relieve Jaws," Nick commanded.

Lolly stood and sprinted away, sending Kelsey up in his place. He must have filled him in on the situation because Kelsey banged through the door looking thunderously angry. He knelt beside the woman and peered closely at her face before adding his own litany of swear words.

"Do you know who this is?" He looked up at Nick who sighed.

"I have some idea, but I was afraid to think it. Is it her?" Nick said.

"It's her," Kelsey said, and somehow Truck knew.

"Shelby Lance?" he guessed.

Kelsey nodded, swiping his hand over his face as he sat back on his heels. Nick remained on watch, but Truck and Kelsey stared at each other over the woman's inert form. Shelby Lance was an American aid worker who had gone missing in Saudi Arabia a month ago. What was she doing here in a whole other country? She was presumed dead, but apparently not. Apparently their target and his men had been having their own sort of fun with her.

"Let's go kill the rest of them," Kelsey said. He picked up the machine gun and prepared to stand. Truck began packing his stuff because for once he and Kelsey were on the same page. Nick wasn't, though.

"No," he said. "Both of you sit down and take a breath. We're here on a mission, one we just completed. We are not vigilante thugs, and it is not our job to mete justice in a country where we're not even supposed to be. Do you know what would happen if it was discovered that four marines killed thirty men in an unoccupied country? Can you say international incident?"

"So, what, you expect us to let them get away with it?" Kelsey said. He and Nick rarely disagreed, but this was definitely one of those times.

"For now, yes. We'll report this and it will go through the proper channels. Then when the decision is made to take action maybe we can be the ones who come back, but we're not going rogue on this assignment," Nick said.

"Is this what it's going to be like now that you're an officer candidate?" Kelsey said. "Are you going soft, worrying about your career?"

Nick's fists clenched, but he remained rooted to the spot. "Believe what you will, but this is still my team and I make the decisions. We're following the law and sticking to our assignment. Besides, who would watch her if we go kill them? Did you think of that? Because I did. Either we would have to leave one of us here to protect her, making it three on thirty, or we would have to leave her alone and unprotected. Which of those scenarios sounds better to you?" Kelsey didn't answer because neither was an acceptable solution, and he was already regretting speaking so rashly. Nick wasn't done, though. "It's going to be hard enough to try and get an injured woman, one they are probably hunting at this very moment, to the pickup zone. That is our new number one priority. We're done talking about this."

Kelsey gave an upward nod. Later, he would have to make amends. But not now because the woman, Shelby, was beginning to stir.

CHAPTER 4

$\mathcal{N}$ick and Kelsey traded places with Kelsey taking watch at the window and Nick kneeling beside the woman. Despite the fact that one of his arms was completely covered in wicked-looking tattoos, women seemed to respond to Nick. His fiancée, Ashleigh, said it was because he had kind eyes, whatever that meant. Truck knew for certain that no one had ever told him *he* had kind eyes. Certainly this woman wouldn't say that, and especially not after he had called her a whore.

He winced, squeezing his eyes closed and taking a breath. Of all the times to be his usual horrible self, why did it have to be then? Why couldn't he have been compassionate like Nick or Lolly, or even funny like Kelsey? Why did he always have to get to the heart of the matter and blurt the worst possible thing?

"Ma'am, I'm Corporal Nick Lassiter, United States Marine Corps. You're with me and my team, and you're safe. Can you tell us your name?"

"Shelby," she whispered. Her throat sounded scratchy and raw. Truck wondered if it was from screaming in pain and fear or simply the dry desert wind. Whatever the reason, he retrieved a bottle of water from his rations and tossed it to Nick who opened it and held it to the woman's lips.

"Can you tell us how you came to be in this country?" Nick asked.

She shook her head. "I don't even know where I am. I was in Saudi Arabia when they kidnapped and drugged me. I woke up in a house a few days later with these men and they…And then we came here. We had just arrived when you shot him, and so I ran."

"How did you find us?" Nick asked.

"I don't know," she said. Her voice was tremulous with unshed tears. "I don't know if I saw something or heard something. All I knew was that the man who had hurt me so much was dead and it was my chance to get away. I hoped rather than guessed that the US was responsible for his death, so I ran to the place where I thought the shot came from."

"But for all you knew it could have been a rival warlord," Truck said and instantly berated himself when Nick shot him a look.

"Better the devil you know, right?" she said, not meeting Truck's gaze. "Only I don't believe that because no one could be worse than the devil I knew. It was…it was bad, and I wasn't a willing participant." This time she glared at Truck.

"We know you were assaulted," Truck said. "And we know it wasn't your fault. I'm sorry." They held each other's gaze for a few seconds before her face relaxed slightly and she looked away.

"I'm sorry you're injured," Nick said in that soothing tone Truck couldn't imitate even if someone was holding a gun to his head. "But I need to know if you think you can walk. We have a chopper coming in forty three hours, and we're going to get you on it, even if we have to carry you."

She flinched, no doubt at the thought of being carried by a man when men weren't her favorite creatures right now. "I can walk," she assured him. "I walked for hours to reach you, but I don't know the last time I ate or drank, and I think maybe I've lost a lot of blood. I'm weak. But I can make it."

"We'll let you rest for a few hours before we get started," Nick assured her. "Drink this water and have some food and then sleep.

You're safe," he reiterated. "None of us will touch you, and we'll be standing guard to make sure no one else does." He retrieved an MRE from his rations, opened it, and held it out to her.

"You're very kind," she said.

"You're an American; it's my job to protect you, and I love my job," he said. Truck thought it was a corny thing to say, but it seemed to make the woman feel better because she smiled and relaxed slightly as she sat back and ate the MRE. And either she believed him that she was safe or she was too exhausted from her ordeal to care because after she finished the food and water she fell asleep.

While she slept, the team had a meeting in the stairwell.

"They're going to follow her, and eventually they're going to find us," Truck pointed out, voicing the words they were already thinking. She was an amateur and had undoubtedly left a trail. The group who had been holding her was paramilitary. At least one of them would have the ability to pick up her scent. They had minutes to hours before they were found, and while they might have enough ammo to make a covert attack, they didn't have enough to hold their ground against thirty hostiles while also protecting an innocent civilian.

"We're going to have to move," Nick said. "And I think we should split up. One of us will take the girl and go to the drop zone while Lolly goes ahead." They were all skilled in camouflage and reconnaissance, but Lolly had a special talent; he was like a ghost, which was why he was such a good point man. He could get in and out without leaving a trace. He was the natural choice to go first and make sure the path was clear.

"One of us will stay with the woman and two will double back and make sure there's no one on our tail," Nick continued. Truck thought it was a good plan because it would protect their front and their flank.

"Which of you is going to stay with the woman?" he asked. He knew it wasn't going to be him; he had already insulted her and she undoubtedly hated him.

"I can do it," Kelsey said. "Something tells me PK wouldn't be okay with you spending that much time with another woman."

"Ashleigh knows I have to do certain things for my job," Nick said, but he still sounded uncomfortable. Women weren't usually a part of their day-to-day operations. Ashleigh was probably more prepared for the prospect of his death than the prospect of him spending three days protecting an attractive woman.

"Why don't you let her choose?" Truck suggested. "That way she's more at ease and, who knows, maybe she'll go for Kelsey." Out of all of them, Kelsey was the one with the movie star good looks. With his outgoing personality, he was rarely without a woman, even though he never got serious with anyone.

"All right," Nick said. "Let's pack it up. Lolly will go on ahead and as soon as she wakes up we roll."

They were adept at packing and erasing any signs of their presence. They swept the house, packing their trash, too. Truck had already given his extra MRE to Shelby, so Lolly, Nick, and Kelsey each gave him their extra and some water. Since they had packed lightly, they had cut it close with the rations, bringing only one extra each. They were cutting it close calorie-wise, but if they made it to the chopper on time they would be fine.

With a nod, Lolly took off and then it was a waiting game as Nick and Kelsey stared at Shelby, willing her to wake up as Truck stood post at the window. For his own amusement, he tried to find Lolly with the scope and couldn't. It was surreal how good the kid was at becoming one with the landscape, especially at night.

"It's going to be dawn soon," he remarked.

"Yeah, we're going to have to wake her," Nick said.

"No, please can we continue to stare creepily for another hour?" Kelsey whispered. "I'm beginning to get my stalker groove on."

"So how are we supposed to wake her?" Nick asked. "I don't want to touch her and freak her out, but obviously the sound of talking isn't going to do it."

Truck left the window, crouched beside the woman, and shook her shoulder. "Shelby, wake up."

She jumped and started to scramble away from him, but he stopped her with a word. "Calm. You're still with the marines, but we need to go. Do you need to use the facilities before we leave? It doesn't flush, so maybe you'd prefer going outside."

"I don't have to go," she said. Her hands trembled, but she was making a concerted effort to pull herself together and not freak out. She sat up, took a deep breath, and let it out slowly.

"Do you need anything we can get you?" Nick asked. On her other side, Kelsey hovered, anxiously biting his lip. Shelby shook her head. "Here's the deal: we're moving out while we're still under the cover of night. We're splitting up the team for maximum coverage. One of us already went ahead as a scout. One is going to stay with you, and two are going to cover the flank. It's up to you which of us you want to accompany you." He pointed between himself and Kelsey. Kelsey gave her a toothy, nervous smile as if being judged worthy for a beauty pageant.

Shelby looked between them and then looked around them. At Truck. "Is it okay if he goes with me?"

No one was as surprised as Truck by the question. Was she suffering some misplaced hero worship because he had carried her up the stairs? But, no, she had been unconscious for that part, and the way she was looking at him wasn't adoring. In fact, she still looked sort of angry at him for the thing he had called her. Maybe that was it; maybe she wanted to be with someone who could be a target for her hapless rage. Either way, Truck didn't want to be "it." He wanted to argue, and Nick knew, so he gave him a look, and that was the end of that.

"Of course you can go with him," Nick said. "We want you to be as comfortable as possible. And you won't ever really be alone; we're going to be within earshot the whole time, even if you can't see us, okay?"

She nodded, looking slightly relieved. "If you're ready, we should probably go," Truck said, fighting down his indignation. He wasn't prepared to keep his pace slow for her or see to her comfort or just plain take care of her. Why did she have to choose him?

"I'm ready." She winced as she sat up. Kelsey put out a hand to help her, but she shied away from him, so he dropped it and backed off.

"Sorry," he murmured, which at any other time and in any other situation would have been funny. Kelsey wasn't one for humility or apologizing. Now, however, it only worked to put them more on edge as they realized anew how alarming the situation was. They didn't merely have a civilian female in their midst; they had one who had been horribly brutalized, meaning they had to treat her with kid gloves. And none of them were less equipped or inclined than Truck. Tamping down his frustration, he grabbed his pack, shouldered his weapon, and waited by the door. She caught up to him and he bounded down the stairs without waiting to see if she was following or needed help.

He stopped when they reached the base of the stairwell. "If I hold up my hand in a closed fist, it means I need you to be silent. If a hold it up like a stop sign, then that obviously means for you to stop. If it's clear, I'll tell you to move forward again like this." He flicked his front two fingers in a come-hither motion. "I don't mean to sound harsh, but if I do any of those things, I need immediate compliance, no questions. You stay beside me at all times. Don't wander off. If you need something, you'll have to let me know. I don't read minds. Ready?"

She nodded once and pressed her lips together. He went first out the door, poking his head around to make sure it was clear even though he knew Lolly was up ahead watching to make sure things were safe. He beckoned her with the signal he had taught her and she cautiously stepped outside, walking quickly to keep pace with him even though he knew she must be in a lot of pain from her injuries. What they had done to her to make her bleed so much he didn't know, and he didn't intend to find out. His focus was to deposit her safely at the hospital in Germany and be on his way. For her sake he hoped her injuries weren't permanent, but that was as deep as he allowed his feelings for her to go. She was another part of the job, another nameless, faceless piece of the human tapestry that made up his life. Civilians on assignments came and went without ever really registering in his psyche.

She kept pace with him as they darted around buildings and burned-out vehicles. This part of the city had been hard hit by the war and even though a lot of time had passed it still resembled a warzone. There was no money or interest in making things better because the cynical feeling of the city's inhabitants was that war would inevitably come again. Why clean things up only to have them destroyed again?

The city afforded its own risks, what with danger having an opportunity for so many convenient hiding places. Soon they would be in the desert, and that opened up a whole new set of problems. They would spend an entire day and night making their way stealthily through the desert until they crossed over the border into a friendlier country, one that looked the other way when American military helicopters landed and took off again.

They reached the edge of the city and took shelter behind one remaining wall of what had once been a restaurant. Truck pulled out a bottle of water and handed it to Shelby, cautioning her to only drink a little because they had to save it for the desert.

"You're all loaded down. What can I carry?" she asked as she took a couple sips and handed the water back.

"Thanks, but we're sort of trained for this type of situation. Everything is so perfectly packed it would be harder to undo it and give it to you."

"If you change your mind, the offer stands," she said. He almost smiled at the hint of pride in her tone. She seemed to be one of those who liked to pull her weight, and he liked that. Even though she was an aid worker, there was always the possibility that she might be a pampered princess who had no idea what she was getting into.

"Did anyone warn you of the dangers of Saudi Arabia?" he asked.

"Yes, but I was staying with family; I thought I was safe."

That's right, she was half Saudi. Her mother had married an American and become a naturalized citizen thirty years ago. "Do you speak Arabic?" Truck asked.

She shook her head. "I have a passion for justice, I guess. Women are always in danger of repression, and I thought if I came and showed them what it means to be an American it might make a difference. Stupid me, I know." She sighed and stared off into the glowing horizon.

"We should go," Truck said. "We're trying to make time while it's night because once that sun comes up, we're going to have to camp out and wait for nightfall again."

"Because it will be so hot?" she asked

"That's one of the reasons," he said. "The other is that we're too easy to spot for any planes doing flyovers. Let's just say we're definitely not supposed to be here."

"Where are we?"

"I can't say," he said.

"You can't tell me where we are?" there was a hint of anger in her tone.

"I'm not allowed to tell you where you are by order of the President of the United States. You try saying no to that," he said.

"Did you come here to save me?" they began walking again, slower this time. He wanted to pick up the pace, but she was hunched forward with her hand draped over her midsection, a clear sign she was in pain even if she wasn't complaining.

"I wish I could say yes, but the answer is no. No one had any idea you were here. The world thinks you're dead." That was probably harsh, but she seemed unfazed. Either she was in shock, or she was really good at dealing with crippling blows.

"What's your name?" she asked.

"Truck," he replied.

"Is that your real name or your nickname?"

"My real name is Ashton," he said. "Ashton Rucker."

"Truck Rucker?" she asked. "How did that happen?"

"My first assignment with the team four years ago was sort of a test run to make sure we jelled. Basically it was a two-man operation and I was window dressing. They made me drive the truck. By the end of day one, that's how they were referring to me. 'Truck, here boy, we need to go over there. Truck, bring the car around, we're ready to leave.'" He shrugged. "The name stuck. It's better than Ashton."

"What's wrong with Ashton? Haven't you ever heard of Ashton Kutcher?"

"That's what's wrong with Ashton," he said. "The only other guy I know of who shares my name is a Hollywood doofus."

"Doofus? You use that word often?"

"I sort of cleaned up my description for your benefit," he said. They walked in silence for a while. Truck pushed up his night vision goggles. Dawn was an insecure time of day where there was too much light for his goggles but not enough light to provide clear vision. The air was beginning to warm, which was good because it had been cold. Shelby was dressed in a robe, a hijab swaddling her head, but there was a chance it might not be warm enough.

"Are those your clothes, or did they dress you that way?" he asked.

"The headscarf is mine. The robes were put on me." She reached down, plucking at them.

"Are you cold?" he asked.

"I'm okay, there's, um, some dried blood, and, um, I'll be glad to change."

"Dried blood is stiff and uncomfortable," he agreed. "Maybe when we stop you can cut out the blood if it's on your undergarments."

"That would be good except that I'm, um, still bleeding quite a lot. If I remove my undergarments, there will be nothing to catch the blood."

His hand clenched on the grip of his gun. He resisted the urge to lash out at her captors, knowing his impotent anger would do nothing to help her now. He almost wished the men who had hurt her were pursuing them so he could kill them all. It was one thing to provoke an attack at their hideout and another to defend themselves in a fight. Maybe they could make their presence known and provoke an attack. There was no doubt he and his team would come away victorious because, even though they were outnumbered, they were better trained than their foes. However, they also had Shelby to think of now. She would no doubt be a target in any firefight and, unlike the four marines, she wasn't wearing camo, a vest, hat, and weapon. Basically, she was a sitting duck. Drawing the bad guys out also meant drawing them to her. Nick was right; retribution would have to wait.

"We're almost done walking," he said. "I need to find some scrub brush, something to provide some shade and cover where we can bunker down."

A few more minutes of walking, and he found what he was looking for, a patch of four scrubby bushes. It wasn't enough to offer shade for both of them, so he would have to build a blind with his tarp, but there was no way they could spend the day uncovered in 118 degree heat. He, at least, had some sun protection built into his uniform. Her hijab offered almost no shelter, something else he needed to keep in mind. And then there were the snakes.

He poked his gun at the bushes, moving them cautiously aside. His first tour in the desert had taught him that snakes like shade, too. It was unlikely they would be there so early in the morning, but always better to be safe than sorry.

"Please don't tell me you're looking for what I think you're looking for," Shelby said.

"I can think of six poisonous snakes in this region off the top of my head," he said. "Six are vipers, and one is a cobra."

She didn't respond, which was odd. Women usually went a little haywire at the mention of snakes. Truck wasn't too fond of them himself. He turned to look at her and noticed her staring off into space, a glazed look on her face. He inclined his head closer and peered at her pupils.

"What are you doing?" she asked, snapping back to the present.

"Checking to see if you're in shock. I expected more of a reaction over the snakes, I guess."

"Have you ever been at such a low point in your life that the possibility of being bitten by a poisonous snake seemed like a step up?" she asked.

"Yes, actually, I have," he said.

She nodded once and resumed staring into space while he arranged a shelter.

"Lie down," he commanded.

"Thanks," she said. She sank to the sand and scooted close to the bushes so he would have maximum shade protection, too. Or she did it to get as far away from him as she could.

"Drink some more water and then get some sleep. When you wake up, we'll eat," he said.

She took the water and drank a few sips before handing it back to him. He was thankful she seemed like a rational person. A more emotional type might have grabbed the water and guzzled to satiate her thirst. Shelby appeared to be thinking it through and conserving their water supply. Or she simply didn't care what happened to her anymore and sipped because she was on autopilot.

He expected her to close her eyes and fall into deep slumber, but she didn't. Instead she remained staring at the tarp over her head. "I haven't cried since it happened. Is that bad? Do you think it means I'm crazy?"

"No." He drank a few sips of water and lay down beside her, being careful not to touch her. "I think it means you're in shock, at least emotionally. It will hit you." He hoped he was away from her when that happened. He hoped she was out of this hellhole where she would have adequate water to supply her tears. It would be painful to cry when her body was too dry to offer up tears as a relief.

"You know why I chose you instead of the other two?" she said.

"No," he said.

"It's because you were the only one who didn't look at me with pity. The whole time it was happening, all I could think was the way everyone was going to look at me from now on. *There's Shelby, the victim. Poor Shelby.* I don't want that. I want to get over this, to move on and live my life again. I'm afraid if I give in and cry, I'll never stop."

"You'll stop," he told her. "Grieving is an important part of the healing process. Don't deny yourself."

"You sound like you have experience with grief," she said.

"Not the kind you're experiencing. No one has ever physically hurt me that way. But I've had my fair share of pain. I wouldn't say I'm the poster boy for mental health, though. It's possible I'm stuck in the anger phase of things."

She actually laughed at that. "You? Nah."

He smiled. "I can't believe it shows when I work so hard to be sweet."

"I like that you tell it how it is. I don't want things to be sugar-coated for me like I'm somehow defective now."

"You should really sleep," he said.

"I know, but I don't think I'll be able to. The ground is uncomfortable, and I can't seem to turn off my brain out here."

"You have to learn to block everything out. Shut down your emotions and that pesky part of you that's reminding you there's sand where there shouldn't be sand. Concentrate on sleep, and it will come. Believe me; I've slept in some pretty amazing positions and situations."

"Like what?" she turned her head to look at him and he did the same so they were inspecting each other, their faces mere inches apart. She was very pretty, even dirty and bedraggled. Her picture had been splashed all over the news before he left the US, so he knew that with only the slightest inducement she was beautiful. He wondered again what had compelled her to come to Saudi Arabia. Curiosity over her mother's homeland? A true desire to help? Or something else?

"I've slept standing up more than once. One time I slept standing up in a swamp with my arms over my head, but only for a minute until my sergeant caught me. I've slept like this, in the desert. Probably the worst was once in Africa where we had to sleep on the grassland. There were lions and tigers. That was the only time I've ever slept somewhere I could actually be eaten. It was odd, fearing a different kind of enemy and a different kind of death." He had zoned out while he talked, lost in his memories. When he focused on her, he expected her to ask what he had been doing in Africa, but she didn't because she was asleep. He watched her for a few minutes, swallowing down a lump of something that felt a whole lot like protectiveness.

He had a protective nature; it was why he was a marine. But this felt like something more than doing his duty to keep someone safe. This felt personal, and it scared him. He didn't want to feel for this woman who was so broken. He had spent the first eighteen years of his life trying to repair someone who was shattered, and it hadn't worked. He didn't have the strength or energy to do it again.

Overhead the sun grew higher and hotter. Truck was in the shade, but still wearing full gear and sweating profusely. It brought back memories of his time in the war but, oddly, the memories were happy. He had been a part of something then. He was a part of something now, but it was different. Then he had been able to share what he was doing with more than three other people. Now he, Lolly, Whit, and Jaws were so far off the radar they almost didn't exist. The feeling was lonelier than he expected.

He blamed Nick for making him realize his loneliness. Everything had been fine before he met Ashleigh and fell in love. Before--with the exception of Lolly who seemed to think women were sacred--Truck and his teammates had been on the same wavelength. Women were nice to have around when you needed or wanted them and expend-able when you didn't. Now Nick was getting *married.* There was a good chance he would soon be someone's dad. Truck didn't feel envy because that path wasn't for him. He couldn't ever devote his life to caring for someone else again; that ship had sailed when his mother offed herself. But he did feel a certain sadness and remorse he couldn't put his finger on. He tried to tell himself it was for the end of their way of life—they would no longer be the fearsome foursome they had once been. But he wasn't sure that was the truth. Maybe his sadness was for himself, a kind of mourning for the life he was giving up by choosing to hold himself in check.

Now there was the added sadness of the true end of their team. With Nick going to Officer Candidate School, Truck, Lolly, and Jaws would undoubtedly be reassigned. They had been lucky to stick together this long. It was unusual that everyone in a scout sniper team was career military, to mention nothing of the miraculous fact that the marines had left them untouched for so long. Shouldn't someone have noticed their happiness by now and given one of them a trans-fer? For the longest time Truck had been waiting for the other shoe to drop because life didn't work out this way, not for him. He wasn't supposed to be happy or feel like a part of a family. Now the thing he had waited for so long had finally happened. His world was being ripped apart, but the fact that he had been correct was a hollow victory in light of everything he would be losing.

His drifting and depressing thoughts were interrupted by the droning of a plane. He squeezed his eyes shut, hating what he was about to do. "Shelby," he said, nudging her with his elbow.

"Hmm." Her eyes flew open and she was instantly on alert and shaking.

"There's a plane."

"Can they see us?"

"No, but there's a good chance they're looking for you, and, if that's the case, then there is also a good chance they're using thermal imaging. I have an insulated cover, but I'm going to have to lie on top of you."

She swallowed hard and clenched her fists at her side to try and stop her trembling. "Is that absolutely necessary?"

"Yes. My suit has built in technology to reduce my infrared silhouette. That, combined with the cover, should be enough to hide me, but not you. I'm going to have to cover you with my body if we have any possibility of avoiding detection. I'm sorry." He spoke even as he pulled the cover from his pack and tucked it around his body.

"Just do it," she said, gritting her teeth and squinting her eyes closed. He covered her and she flinched.

"I would never hurt you," he said, aiming to mimic Nick's soothing tone.

"Rationally I know that, but it's not only the feel of your body. It's your smell. The body odor triggers my memories of them, and I…I'm panicking. I want to buck you off and run away. Oh, God, please help me."

He was fairly certain the last part was an actual prayer because she was having a full-on panic attack. If he didn't get her calmed down, there was a real danger that she might do what she threatened, throw him off, and run from the shelter. "You know how I thought you were a hooker at first?" he said. The harsh words momentarily jogged her out of her panic. She opened her eyes and looked at him in wary surprise. "It's because my mother was a prostitute. The way those men looked at you, I could tell what they had done to you. It was the same way the men in town used to look at my mother. Imagine what it was like when I was a little kid to go to the store and be able to tell who was using my mom. It was a real shocker when I saw my middle school principal give her the look. Talk about awkward. No wonder I was in trouble all the time; I hated his guts."

"Your mom was a prostitute?" she whispered.

"Yep. Not just a prostitute, but *the* prostitute. We were from this real small town where everyone knows everyone. Other kids' moms were the banker's wife, the teacher, the housewife. My mom was the town whore. Career day was lots of fun."

She licked her parched lips. "You said 'was.' Did she get cleaned up, get her life straightened around?"

He debated not telling her, but now that the story was pouring out of him, he couldn't seem to stop. He had never told anyone the details of his life before. Maybe he was lonelier than he thought, or maybe he sensed a resounding brokenness in her. "No. I came home from basic and found her swinging from a rope in my room. She must have really hated me to do it that way, where she was sure I would be the one to find her."

"Maybe not," Shelby said. "Maybe she wasn't thinking rationally and she wanted the pain to end. And maybe she wanted to do it in the one place where she felt closest to you, the one place where the love was able to break through the pain and give her a moment of peace before she went."

He stared at her as something inside him, a pain he had been harboring the last nine years, finally broke free and fluttered away. Before finding her in his room, he would have sworn his mother loved him. She took care of him as best she could, despite her raging mental illness and dependence on him. She was affectionate. She *told* him she loved him. But he had taken that final act as proof that she hadn't loved him at all. Now Shelby had given him a new perspective. Maybe his mother really had loved him. Maybe going to his room had been one last desperate way to try and reach out to him, to try and let his love surround her and give her an ounce of peace in her tortured life.

"It's okay," Shelby said. He didn't realize he was crying until she spoke and touched her fingertips to his cheek, wiping away his tears. His mouth opened—to try to explain or apologize?—but no sound came out. Instead he simply cried. She moved her hand to the back of his head and tugged him closer until his head rested on her chest and still he didn't stop crying. He gave in for a few precious minutes, letting the tears wash away a little of the gnawing pain. It was nowhere near emptied when he sat up abruptly, moving away from her as he strained to listen for the sound of the airplane.

"It's gone," he said, rolling off her and removing the stifling thermal liner. "I'm so sorry. That was uncalled for and unprofessional." He couldn't look at her. He had never been more humiliated. He had allowed himself to lose it on the job. Not only that, but he had allowed a civilian to comfort him, someone who had been through her own harrowing trauma.

"It's really okay," she said. He ignored her as he repacked the thermal cover. "Ashton," she said, using his formal name to catch his attention. "It's really okay. I...I sort of needed that. It was nice to be taken out of my own grief for a minute, to realize I have something to offer someone else. And, to use some of that brutal honesty you love, it's nice to know I'm not the only one who's damaged."

"Yeah, welcome to the club. We meet on Mondays, but you'd better bring your own food because the fatties get there first and eat it all," he said.

She smiled. "Whoa, you have a sense of humor underneath all the angry. Who knew?"

"I don't get to use it much around Kelsey--he's the tall one you met at the house. He's our resident comedian, or so he believes. No one is as funny as he thinks he is." He rolled his eyes and her little smile blossomed until it lit her face, erasing a little of the grief.

"Why don't you take a turn sleeping now?" she suggested.

He shook his head. "I won't sleep till we're out of here. You go back to sleep. We have a long night of walking ahead of us."

"The other guys, they're watching over us, right?" she asked.

"We're as safe as we can be except for the planes."

"I know what those sound like now. I'll keep watch. You sleep."

"I…" he started to protest, and then caught sight of her expression. She was apparently the type of woman who liked to take care of others. It meant a lot for her to be able to do this one thing for him and, honestly, he didn't expect the plane to come back for hours, if it came back at all. If they had been looking for her, they wouldn't expect her to be with soldiers who would hide her thermal image. Since they had swept the area, they would most likely move on and look elsewhere. And with Lolly in the front and Kelsey and Nick in the back, they were covered and safe. There was no reason for him not to sleep except for his own pride. But he could bend his pride if it meant taking her out of her grief again and making her feel good about something, at least for a little while.

"All right," he said. "Keep an ear out for planes, and also watch for snakes and scorpions."

"If I see a snake, do I have your permission to shoot it?" she asked.

"No. Don't touch my gun." As if to make sure she wouldn't, he hugged it to his chest, rolled up in the fetal position, and fell asleep.

CHAPTER 5

"Why did you really go to Saudi Arabia?"

He slept, and then she slept, and now they were eating and killing time before they resumed their hike.

"I told you. To be a shining example of American freedom for the women there," she said.

"I don't believe you," he replied. "That sounds like the reason you memorize to tell people, the one that looks good on paper. What's the real reason?"

She wrinkled her nose, whether at him or at the container of MRE macaroni and cheese he didn't know. "Perceptive, aren't you?"

"I'm trained to be," he replied. "So what is it? Were you secretly hoping to meet a rich Saudi husband? It's usually about a man, isn't it?"

"Not anymore," she said.

He winced and opened his mouth to apologize before stifling the urge. She wanted to be treated like normal; he wouldn't spend his time apologizing for normal conversation. "So what, then?"

"My mom is a doctor, and my dad has a doctorate; he's a professor. They're both a big deal."

He frowned. Was she putting him down because he was a marine who lacked a college education? She was so approachable he had sort of forgotten her family's notoriety.

"I'm the youngest in my family. Everyone else is pursuing their doctorate or MD or already has it. And then there's me. I'm severely dyslexic. School was a nightmare. I squeaked through by the skin of my teeth, and I hated every minute of it. My family, they say all the right words you're supposed to say when someone has a learning disability. 'It's okay, Shelby. We understand. Do your best. We're here for you.' So maybe I'm crazy or paranoid, but I never felt like they meant it. It always seemed as if they felt like if I only tried hard enough, I could overcome my problems. If I studied harder, listened more, took better notes, then I could do as well as them. But I couldn't. Do you know how it feels to try your hardest at something and still be an epic failure?"

"Yeah, actually, I do," he said. He had tried his hardest to help his mother, and he had failed in the worst possible way.

"I guess you do," she said, sighing. "So I thought if I couldn't be smart at least I could be passionate. I could be an activist like my mother. I came here and at first it felt so great. I shocked everybody. I think they thought I was going to be living off their coattails forever, or maybe welfare. Let's say my last job before I came here included saying the words 'Do you want fries with that?' a whole lot. For one brief, shining moment they were proud of me. I was being courageous and brilliant. I had a cause." She looked toward the setting sun and shook her head. "And now I'm coming home worse off than I ever was. Typical Shelby. At least I really know how to fail. I don't fail little; I fail on an epic scale. Not content to be raped by one terrorist thug, I have to be gang raped by a whole group of them." She pressed her closed fist to her mouth. He wondered if she was trying not to cry or trying not to throw up. For his own part, he felt like doing a little of both.

"You know what? Forget them. If they can't accept you for who you are, then write them off and move on."

"You can't write off your family," she said.

"You can. It's not easy, and it's not always the best solution, but if they're the type of people who are going to make you feel bad for being raped, then forget them. Make a new family. See your original family on holidays. Play the part of the dutiful daughter and show up. But don't make yourself vulnerable to attack."

"You know you're the first person who has ever suggested such an audacious thing to me, and it feels so good." She pressed her fist to her mouth again, afraid she may have said too much. "I can't do that, though. They're good people, nice people. They don't mean to make me feel the way I do. It's my problem, not theirs."

"Then you have to deal with it the best way you can. You're the only one who can protect yourself. Make it happen. Figure out what you need to change the situation and do it. Unless you don't want to change, unless you like being the family screw-up."

"I don't," she said, her tone vehement. "Who would?"

"Maybe *like* is a strong word. Maybe you're complacent in that role because it's what you know. But it doesn't have to be. Leaving my mom to become a marine was the hardest thing I ever did, but I needed to do it, and I'm glad I did. Without the corps, I would be dead by now. You need to find your corps, whatever it may be. Find what works for you and do it, no excuses."

"You realize you sound like a motivational promo for the marines," she said, grinning.

He began an off-key rendition of the Marine Hymn and she put her hands over her ears.

"Okay, stop. That would definitely drive any prospective marines away," she said.

He smiled, tucking their trash into his pack. They had to be careful to leave no traces of their presence. American water bottles and MRE's were certainly a glowing red flag that soldiers had been in the area. "We should probably get going now that the sun is down. Plus, it's going to get really cold soon. Walking will feel good."

"If you say so," she said. "I thought I was in shape from Pilates, but walking in the sand is making me rethink that."

"It's almost over. One more night and day. Then another night and we should reach the rendezvous point by morning, and the chopper will be here sometime after that." He didn't tell her how much faster they had made it without her. They had been dropped at the same place and run all through the night to make their destination. Plodding slowly was excruciating, but a necessity for her sake.

"You know what's weird? I'm kind of not looking forward to that. I feel like I've found a small measure of peace and security with you. I don't want to have to start all over with a new group of men and rehash everything when I get to the hospital."

"The soldiers who retrieve us don't have to know anything about what's happened to you. We'll only be with them for a few hours until we reach Germany. And the doctors there are good; they're compassionate. I've landed myself there a time or two for various ailments," he said.

"I notice you didn't say you'll stay with me," she murmured. "It's ridiculous to think you would I just…I would like that, to feel like I have a friend."

Truck expected to feel some fear at her words. After all, wasn't this what he had been dreading? Somehow she had worked her way behind his defenses and become more than a nameless, faceless civilian. But he couldn't seem to muster any fear, only regret because Germany would be the end of the road for them.

"I'm sorry," he said. "Our assignment doesn't include staying for any length of time. We'll have to drop you and go, but I promise you'll be in good hands. And you can write; we can stay in contact." It might be nice to have a sort of pen pal. She lived in Texas, so it wasn't as if they would be seeing each other ever again.

"Have you ever had a letter from a dyslexic?" she asked. "People will see it, and they'll be like, 'Aw, who's the little kid who's writing to you, Truck? Your niece?'"

He laughed, sure she was exaggerating. "And I'll say, 'No, it's my friend, Shelby. She's awesome. She's the only dyslexic in a family of geniuses, which makes her kind of special.'"

"You know what I like about you, Ashton? It's that you're a secret optimist with a can-do attitude. By all rights, you should be as grumpy as you seem, but you're not. Talk about special."

They walked in silence a few minutes. Truck was wary because dusk was as insecure as dawn. There was too much light for his night-vision equipment, but too many shadows to see clearly.

"Ashton," Shelby said. Her tone was tentative. He took his eyes off the horizon to glance at her. "I was thinking about something. Maybe this time with you is kind of a blessing, you know? The forced togetherness is like immersion therapy. It was only a few days ago that I thought I would never let another man get within ten feet of me, let alone touch me, and yet I did. It wasn't easy, but I did it. Maybe I'm supposed to use this time to begin the healing process, to help get over my fear of men. So I was wondering if maybe, if you don't mind, and if you do it's okay, but would it maybe be okay if I could hold your hand?"

At first he was a little speechless by her request because he knew how much it cost her. She didn't want to hold his hand. She was making herself do it, to take a first step toward where she didn't want to go—intimacy with a man. She was on his right side, though, which would never do because he was right-handed and his gun was in that arm. So he reached over his body with his left hand, clasped her hand, and pulled her to his left side, their hands dangling between them.

"Thanks," she said.

He smiled down at her even though it was probably too dark to see now. The sun had a way of dropping suddenly out of sight in the desert. He let her go to pull down his goggles and then picked up her hand again, giving it a squeeze. "I can only imagine what my teammates must be thinking of this little scene," he said.

She laughed again, a miracle because she didn't have a lot to laugh about right now. "Maybe they'll think you're so incredibly suave you somehow got around my roadblocks and gained a little ground. You could be the stuff of legends."

"If they thought I was hitting on you, they would make their presence known and beat the, uh, stuffing out of me." Editing his words was a little easier for him since meeting Nick's fiancée, Ashleigh. She didn't curse and, though she had never judged them for doing so, being around someone like her had a natural tendency to make one watch his mouth. He was finding that Shelby had the same effect on him.

"They seem very nice," she commented.

"They're family," he said. "Spending so much time together and surviving so many crazy things has a way of doing that to you. I count them as brothers."

They walked in silence awhile, their joined hands swinging gently between them as if they were teenagers strolling through a mall instead of two adults tromping through the sand.

"Ashton," she ventured.

"Mmm."

"Did you ever notice that sometimes when you're walking in silence it sort of opens up your brain to everything you're trying hard not to think about?"

"Yes," he said. He had been thinking the same thing before he met her.

"I guess what I'm trying to say is that I know you're not a naturally chatty person, and you're already doing so much by rescuing me. But when you talk, I really listen because your life is fascinating. So maybe if it's not too much trouble you could talk and distract me for a while?"

It sort of was a lot to ask. She was right; he wasn't naturally a chatty person, especially not about himself—a topic that was painful no matter which way he approached it. And they were walking. He was parched, even though the sun had gone down. But in the grand scheme of things, it was nothing at all. Surely he could do this one thing for her, surely he could think of something to say that wasn't dreary or dire.

"Nick is getting married," he blurted. Marriage was a topic most women loved, and Shelby appeared to be no exception. He sensed rather than saw her smile.

"Oh yeah? When?"

"They haven't set a concrete date yet. He's going to Officer Candidate School—that's in Virginia. It lasts a few months. Probably sometime after he gets back."

"Are you in the wedding?"

"We all are, me, Kelsey, Lolly, Melly."

"Melly? Who is Melly?"

"She's Lolly's sister."

"Is she your girlfriend?"

That was such a startling question that he paused to look at her before answering. "No why would you think that?"

"Something in your tone. It got sort of softer, the way men talk about the woman of their dreams," Shelby said.

Truck frowned. He didn't like to think of himself as softening toward any woman, even Melly. Maybe especially not Melly. "Melly is a nice person," he said, choosing his words carefully. "She's a nice woman. The first woman I've trusted in my adult life."

"So why don't you date her?" Shelby asked.

A rock whizzed by Truck's head, and he bit back a laugh. Apparently Kelsey was closer than he realized. "Let's say she's spoken for, and it's not like that with us. We're friends. I don't want to date anyone. Ever."

They strolled in silence a few minutes more before she spoke. "I guess we're sort of in the same boat again. It's odd how your life can change on a dime, isn't it? A month ago I thought the worst thing that could happen to me was being asked on a date by my cousin. And now that seems like a mild anecdote in comparison."

"You didn't have a boyfriend in the states?" He found that hard to believe; she was a beautiful woman, and, from what he knew of her, she had a pleasant personality, too.

"No. I've never really dated beyond the ubiquitous prom and homecoming in high school."

"Why not?" he asked. "You're pretty."

She chuckled. "Thank you. It's not often a woman gets to hear she's pretty when she looks her absolute worst. To answer your question I guess I never found what I was looking for. I know that sounds corny, but it's true. I was a tomboy in school, one of those girls who is friends with all the guys. I've never been good at the dating game— flirting, chasing, being pursued. I always wanted to marry my best friend, but as hard as I tried, I couldn't make myself fall in love with my best friend. He has a serious girlfriend now, and our relationship has kind of dwindled. Not that I can blame him. I mean, it's weird to be close friends with one woman when you're trying to woo another."

"I can't believe I'm about to ask this, but you've piqued my curiosity. What are you looking for in a guy? What are you searching for that's so hard to find?" He didn't understand what she was getting at. In his world, you hooked up with someone or you didn't. There was no standing back to make sure they fit into your lifestyle beforehand. Of course, that philosophy might also explain why he had never had a serious girlfriend.

"Character, integrity, intelligence. I know that's sort of hypocritical of the person with the learning disability to require intelligence, but there are all kinds of smart. I don't want a scholar—indeed, I would prefer not—but someone who is smart is a must."

Her accent was mesmerizing, as was her turn of phrase. Being from the south, he was used to southern accents. Her Texas drawl was slightly different from his twang, but some of her words were clipped, leading him to believe she had been more influenced by her Saudi mother than she realized. She sounded a little like the locals who spoke English. No matter how well they spoke, there was always that little trace of accent.

"In all your twenty four years you've never been able to find a man who meets your criteria?" he asked, incredulous.

"I've been interested in people, but the men I like tend to be as intimidated by my family as I am. And for the last few years I've been drifting, trying to find my way, trying to find a path. It didn't seem like a good time to drag someone else along for the journey of discovery."

"I respect that," Truck said, adding a decisive nod of his head. "Some women think a man can solve all their problems, and then resent him when he can't."

"Not me. I'm too messed up for any man to fix. Always have been." She darted him a wry smile that was tinged with immeasurable sadness. "Always will be," she added, half under her breath.

"I don't think that's true," Truck said. "I'm a cold-hearted cynic, and yet I like you. I believe in you. I think you can go home and turn this little tragedy into triumph." He shook his head. "That sounded like something from a motivational poster, sorry."

Shelby chuckled. "No, don't apologize. It's up there with the ten nicest things anyone has ever said to me, above my cousin who told me I have good hips for childbearing, I'll have you know."

He whistled appreciatively. "I'm surprised anything can top that one." His eyes swept her up and down, noting the hunched set of her shoulders, the hand that wasn't holding his draped over her midsection. "Shelby, how's the pain?"

"I assume you're asking about my physical wellbeing and not the untapped well of psychic misery," she said, aiming for a cheerful tone that came off strained. "I'm making it."

"We can stop; we can rest."

"It's better if we don't. If I stop, I'm afraid I may never get started again. The only thing that's keeping me plodding forward is the distraction you're offering, so thank you. Now, back to Nick and his pending wedding. Tell me all you know. How did they meet? Is she a marine?"

"Close. Her name is Ashleigh. They met when she accidentally shot him."

Her reaction didn't disappoint. Her step faltered in surprise, and he gripped her hand tighter, holding her upright. "This is going to be good, I know it. Start from the beginning and tell me everything."

He started with what he knew of Nick and Ashleigh's relationship, which wasn't much. He had kept his nose to himself, preferring not to watch Nick make a wreck of his life by tying himself down so young. If he had thought he would someday have to give an injured companion all the details, he would have paid better attention.

"I take it you don't approve," Shelby said.

Truck cleared his throat, uncomfortable with the knowledge that Nick was most likely listening in. "It's not the life I would have chosen, but it's not really my business."

"Is he happy?"

"Disgustingly so," Truck replied. He heard a faint sound that may have been Kelsey stifling a laugh.

"So is it the woman? Do you not like Ashleigh?"

He had to think about that, which made him feel sort of bad for Nick's listening ears. But he was relieved when the answer came. "I do," he said.

"Why do you sound so surprised?" Shelby asked.

"She's religious," Ashton said, wrinkling his nose as if he had announced Ashleigh had bedbugs.

"Is she one of those who shoves it down your throat? Does she constantly proselytize?"

"No, nothing like that. She would never."

"Then why does it bother you?" she asked.

"I don't know." He was feeling frustrated trying to put words to things he had only ever sensed before. "It's not her, I guess; it's God. We're not on the best of terms."

"You don't believe in God?" she asked, incredulous as she looked up at him.

"It's not that I don't believe," he said. It was hard to make it through childhood in the south without at least a glancing acquaintance with God and church. When he was really little, there was a church in town that reached out to him and used to pick him up for church every Sunday with a big blue school bus. He had loved going to church then and had sat by the window every week, his little face pressed against the glass. When had that changed? When had he stopped going? When had he lost what little faith he ever had? "It's just, what has He done for me lately, you know?"

"Well, you're alive," Shelby said. "And I don't mean that in a flippant way like we should all give thanks we're alive every day. But I bet you've faced death more times than anyone on the planet. And yet you're still here. That's something."

Yes, that was something. There had been some close calls, too many to count. First in the war and then on the crazy, impossible missions this team sometimes performed. He supposed he owed a grudging gratitude for his life, such as it was. "Doesn't what you went through make you think that maybe if He's up there, then He's not listening? I mean, you can't tell me you didn't pray for it not to happen." Belatedly he realized it was a typically insensitive thing to say to someone who had been so recently traumatized, proving he lacked the sensitivity gene completely.

Shelby seemed undaunted by his bluntness, however. "I did pray. And then I was rescued by you." She gave him a pointed, triumphant glance.

"But after it was already too late," Truck said.

"God is not a genie in a bottle. If He was, what would be the point? If it was easy, if believing and praying saved you from every bad thing, of course everyone would want to believe and follow. It would be like magic. The point is not to believe only when things are going well, but when they're going bad, too. Do I wonder why this happened to me? Yes. Do I wish it hadn't? Yes. Do I blame God? No. There's evil in the world, but good, too. You guys, for example. You're like a shining beacon of bravery and goodness after the cesspool I've been living in. You may not believe in God, but He believes in you, and He's using you with or without your consent."

Truck frowned, not sure he liked that thought at all. Shouldn't he have to give his consent to be part of some bigger plan? He didn't like giving up control of his life, but if what Shelby said was true, then control was an illusion anyway. "But that seems even crueler, like we're all puppet s in some play."

"That's one way of looking at it I suppose," she conceded. "But what if it's the best play ever written? What are the odds we would both be in a country where neither of us is supposed to be at exactly the right time? And what are the chances I saw whatever I saw that alerted me to your presence? And how likely is it that I found you on my own, traipsing through a burned out city full of hostiles who would kill me for being an American woman? And yet here we are. I found you, you saved me, and we're holding hands walking through the desert, talking about life's deepest subjects. Seems a little too coincidental to be mere chance," she said.

"Time for a break," Truck announced, coming to an abrupt halt. He pulled out a bottle of water and handed it to her. She sipped and handed it back. There was an awkward sort of tension between them now, probably caused by Truck's discomfort. For years he had avoided deep topics, pushing them to the back of his mind whenever they arose. He functioned on sheer numbness—anything else was too dangerous. But Shelby's words were beginning to crack his carefully constructed outer shell.

There was a time when he was young, before the marines, before his mother's death, that he had been a sensitive and shy boy, the kind who cried over an injured bird on the sidewalk. He had hidden his tears, even from his mother, but he had cried. But then the hurts became too many and too deep. He stopped crying, stopped feeling anything at all. Now occasionally a little bit of anger worked its way to the surface, but anger was good; anger was fuel. Sadness, longing, and loneliness—they were his death knell, the undoing of all that he had worked so hard to create over the last decade. No longer was he Ashton Rucker, piteous son of the town whore. Now he was Truck, calm and tough machine gunner for the United States Marines. The few, the proud, the brave—Truck had bought it all, adapting to his new identity like a fish that has lived out of water its whole life and finally comes home. The marines gave him the identity he had been longing for, and he wasn't about to risk an emotional breakdown now.

Shelby had the look of someone who knew she had offended, but had no idea how. "Ashton," she began, but he interrupted her.

"You can call me Truck," he said.

"Oh. Okay." She bit her lip and looked away. The palpably wounded expression proved to Truck that he was the biggest heel the world had ever known. How could he hurt her of all people? And now of all times? He might as well take a wrecking ball to what little self-preservation she had left. He felt his heart starting to soften toward her again, and hefted his pack onto his shoulders before the misplaced sympathy could gain a foothold.

"We should get going," he said, his tone clipped and frustrated.

She began walking again. This time they didn't hold hands.

CHAPTER 6

"*D*id you know that about Truck's mom?"

They weren't supposed to be talking, but Kelsey had barely ever managed that. Even when it was a life-or-death scenario, he was usually mouthing something to himself. Nick shook his head, probably in a futile attempt to warn Kelsey away from further conversation. The warning was lost on him, but he was too lost in his thoughts to say more for the moment. Truck's mom had been a hooker. Not only that, but she had killed herself and left him to find her. That certainly explained a lot about Truck's seeming hatred of women.

Kelsey felt an odd sort of resentment because Truck had never told them before. They had told each other everything, or so Kelsey thought. There was certainly nothing about his life he had left unshared. He thought it was the same with everyone else, but now he had his doubts. Was there anything Nick and Lolly hadn't told him? As always, he heard Melly's voice in his head, reminding him it wasn't all about him. It was true that he was a bit needy and clingy, but wasn't that the purpose of friendships—to provide each other's needs? Granted, his needs were greater than most. He was the first to admit he was an enigma. How he could be both cocky and insecure baffled even him, but there it was. He had no doubt about his good looks or his many talents. He had no doubt people loved him. His doubt was over whether they loved him *enough*. Did they love him enough not to leave him? That was always the big question. His whole life, everyone had left in one way or another—usually through death. First his parents and then his beloved grandmother. He wasn't willing to lose anyone else. His circle was small, but he intended to hold it together even if he had to do so with clutched hands and bleeding fingertips.

The sun began to rise. Truck and the girl made camp, which meant Kelsey and Nick could do the same. He chose his own suitable spot, close enough that he would be able to eavesdrop should they ever start to talk again, but far enough away that he wouldn't be spotted.

The sun burst into view, along with the heat. He would never get used to the way it went from hot to cold and back again with no in between. His mind was scrambling, trying to provide reasons he shouldn't sleep. Nick was on watch for the first part of the day, which meant it was Kelsey's turn to rest. But it remained elusive as his mind kept running over all the things he had learned about his teammate today. At least he knew someone else doubted God's existence as much as he did. With Nick's marriage had come a total change, and Lolly was Lolly—their devout little priestling.

To try and coax himself to sleep, Kelsey had the daydream, the one he had perfected over the years, the one he would never in a million years tell Melly about because she was the star. Not that she was doing anything out of the ordinary in the dream because she wasn't. She simply fed him a bowl of her homemade flan while she talked to him and ran her fingers through his hair. In real life, these were probably things he could persuade her to do if he begged hard enough, though not without a whole lot of grumbling on her part. And it wasn't even the bikini she always wore in this vision because he had taken that from real life. He had shown up at her house unannounced once and caught her sunbathing in her backyard, her cherry-red bikini a far cry from the modest one piece she always wore when they went to the ocean. The bikini had been a delightful revelation, one that he cherished. She was definitely the only one of his friends he ever wanted to see in a bikini. That wasn't what held him back from revealing his frequent deployment fantasy to her, however. He wasn't sure why he didn't want to tell her; he just didn't. It was his private dream and he didn't have to share it. He left it at that and finally fell asleep.

* * *

Shelby had messed up everything with her inability to keep her mouth shut. In her defense, it was hard to keep a muzzle on her mouth when her energy was being diverted elsewhere—namely to trying to hold herself together. Maybe she should go for the gold and bring up politics with Ashton—no, Truck—and then she would have broken all the rules of polite conversation. Why did she have to talk about her beliefs after he said he didn't like the other woman, Ashleigh, for the same reason? Maybe it was because she was trying to puzzle it out for herself. This was the first truly bad thing that had ever happened to her in her life, apart from her dyslexia and disappointing family situation. She was trying to react with faith she didn't quite feel at the moment, trying to search for rainbows in a sky so cloudy it appeared black. After all, if she didn't have her faith, then what did she have?

The painful silence gave her lots of time to think about that question. She wasn't smart or talented. She had nothing but a pretty face and sunny disposition to see her through. Where was she if her sunny disposition went away? Just another pretty face? And what had that ever done for her when she had no idea how to use it? But was abiding faith the same thing as a sunny disposition? Were happiness and joy the same? If not, then how did she attain joy now when everything was so bleak and her life was in shambles? She hated having more questions than answers when a couple of months ago she thought she had everything all figured out. Maybe she hadn't, though. Maybe she had been happy because she had never been tested. Only now that she was being tested, she had no energy for optimism; she had no energy for anything.

She was hot, miserable, uncomfortable, and in pain. All day there had been a fine trickle of blood running down her leg. What had they done to her to make her bleed so? Was she permanently damaged? Would she ever be able to have kids?

She had to press her fist to her mouth and stifle her explosive emotions with that thought. She longed for children, even more than she wanted a husband. She had already decided that she would adopt someday, take in the kids no one else wanted and be a mother to their friends, too. She had always had a heart for the disenfranchised. Perhaps that was what drew her to Truck, and not his adamant refusal to pity her. Maybe in him she had sensed a wounded soul. Though they had come from two different worlds, shattered souls seemingly had a way of finding each other, even in the middle of nowhere.

The sun was barely up, and it was beginning to chase away the lingering chill from her bones. Shelby knew the desert was hot during the day, but she hadn't counted on the freezing nights. The lack of humidity in the air kept it from retaining any heat, so as soon as night fell it was immediately cold, so cold she now felt a little like a lizard sunning itself on a rock. She was immobilized from the cold and stiffness in her body. Unfortunately there was only a short window before the sun turned from comforting to sweltering. But for now, for these few blessed moments, the sun felt immensely good. Shelby closed her eyes and soaked up the rays while Truck arranged the shelter around her. She should move. Or help him. Anything but lie there like an invalid with her eyes closed, but her energy was gone. How he was able to keep moving despite the mind-numbing cold and exhaustion was inspiring, and also a little guilt-inducing. True, he was doing his job. And, unlike her, he wasn't injured. But none of those rationalizations made her feel like any less of a helpless victim.

She opened her eyes and looked up at him. "Is there anything I can do to help?"

"No." His tone was clipped. Apparently he was still freezing her out. She resisted the urge to sigh. It shouldn't hurt so much, the rejection of this near-stranger, but he was the only person she knew for thousands of miles. Though there were three other men nearby, she neither saw nor heard them. It was as if she and Ashton were alone. She had been alone for the last month, struggling to survive. She didn't want to be alone again.

He lay down beside her and propped his head on his gun. It must have been a ridiculously uncomfortable position, but maybe that was the point because he didn't look like he was going to be sleeping anytime soon. He stared at the scrub-covered shelter above them, as silent and cool as a corpse.

"I'm sorry," Shelby said, and she really meant it. "I shouldn't have brought up the stuff about religion. I shouldn't have pushed you to talk and distract me. That was an unfair burden to place on your already overloaded shoulders." She would have gone on, but he interrupted her.

"Don't," he said. "I'm not mad at you, Shelby. I'm an all-around miserable human being. Our conversation today reminded me of that fact, and I took out my feelings on you. I'm the one who is sorry."

There was so little inflection in his voice that he might have been talking about the weather, but she knew he meant the words. One of her friends from back home was the same way. Whenever he was angry at himself, he took it out on everyone else. He was a real pain sometimes. She wanted to tell Ashton this, to make another connection with him, but she was afraid to put herself out there, to push him further than he wanted to go. Obviously it was important to him to maintain whatever emotional walls he had built. At least she thought so until his hand inched over and clasped hers in comforting, reassuring embrace.

Strangely, it was that small touch that triggered the crack in her defenses. The tears welled so fast behind her eyes they felt like someone jabbed her with a fist. With effort, she swallowed down the sobs, saving them for another day, another time. Ashton had enough emotional baggage of his own without adding hers. The least she could do was spare him the additional burden of having to comfort a hysterical female.

His thumb smoothed over her fingers. Since he seemed lost in his own thoughts, she thought it was an unconscious gesture on his part.

Whether he intended it to be or not, it was intensely comforting. She focused hard, sending all her pain and discomfort to those four fingers, allowing every gentle pass of his thumb to ease a tiny bit of her grief and misery. After a few minutes of pretending, she was fast asleep.

* * *

WHEN SHE WOKE a few hours later, he was still predictably awake. "You should get some rest, Ashton," she said. She bit her chapped lip, belatedly remembering she was supposed to call him Truck now, but he didn't comment or seem disturbed by her lapse.

"I'm all right." His accent was in full force. The first time he spoke to her, she had no idea he was from the south, so straight was his speech. She wondered what the catalyst was for his on-again, off-again accent. For her, she tended to drawl more when she was with her family or friends, people she was comfortable with. She didn't think that was the case with Ashton, though. Surely he didn't feel so comfortable or familiar with her after his angry outburst informing her he wanted nothing to do with her. "How are you?" he added.

"I'm all right," she said, adding more inflection to her accent to mimic him.

He smiled. "Are you making fun of me, little miss?"

"No, sir," she said, and now their smile was conspiratorial, a recognition of being mutually southern with all that it implied. They were very near each other—a necessity under the shelter that was only meant for one person. He was pressed against the length of her from shoulder to foot. A couple of days ago she would have felt physically ill at such contact, but now there was a sort of comforting reassurance in his presence. Somewhere along the way he had unwittingly won her complete trust. He wouldn't hurt her; to the contrary, he would probably give his life to protect her, not only because it was his job, but because it was the type of person he was.

She studied his face in such close proximity to hers. He was a handsome man. His hair was tawny brown, his eyes a similar shade.

They were deeply set and small which could make him look shrewd or standoffish, but right now they were warm and kind. He had a rather pale complexion, despite what must be endless hours in the sun. His nose was perfect and straight, his lips slightly pursed. He looked like a painting of an eighteenth century noble come to life, only she guessed he was more ripped than any nobleman had ever been.

While she was making her inspection, he was making one of his own. He was concerned about her. Lolly was the one with the medical training, but it was impossible to have been in the field so long and not picked up a few things. Her pupils were slightly slow to react, her respirations becoming a bit shallow. Combined with her listlessness, Truck thought maybe she was becoming dehydrated. She was pale despite her dark complexion, her cheeks looking sallow, her eyes hollow. It was bad enough that they were in the desert with limited provisions, but she was also injured and the last he knew she was still bleeding. And then there was her emotional trauma. Where she was getting her reserves was a mystery to him. He had been in the marines for almost a decade, and he had seen everything. But rarely had he seen civilians with as much grit and determination as she was show-ing. Experience told him that she should be a weeping, hysterical mess right now. He wouldn't be surprised if they needed to take turns carrying her. Instead she was calm, a repressed smile playing hide and seek on her lips. It wasn't often he met people who surprised him in a good way, but Shelby was definitely one of those people. He hated to think that she might someday turn bitter over her ordeal, that the trauma of what she had been through would wear away her bloom of innocence and sweetness. He picked up her hand and squeezed it, as if he could somehow convey these thoughts and wishes to her.

That was another thing to marvel over. When had he last held hands with a woman? Holding hands was a gesture of affection and intimacy, a way to link two people together. In all of his adult life, he had never wanted to establish that sort of intimacy or tenderness with a woman. He had eschewed intimacy, searching instead for women who were content to spend a few days with a marine. There were always plenty to be found, and certainly no groupies inspired the sort of feelings he was having now, feelings of protectiveness and friendship, of caring about another human being besides himself, his teammates, and Melly.

Trust didn't come easily to him. Even his teammates had taken almost a year to worm their way behind his defenses. Melly, by virtue of being a woman, had taken longer. And here was Shelby, standing equal among them after only a few days. The thought should have terrified him, but it didn't. For the first time in a long time, it felt good to lower his guard a little, to let someone in, to focus on someone else's problems and cares for a while.

His last attempt at rejecting her had been too painful for them both, and he was done trying to shut her out. She needed someone and, by whatever cosmic joke, he was the person sent to see her through. Her heartfelt and sad little apology for unconsciously offending him had been the shattering element against his paltry defenses. Until he handed her off to the hospital in Germany, he determined to be a real friend to her, whatever that meant. Even if it ripped open his carefully concealed emotional baggage, even if her departure left fresh wounds on top of old ones. For once it wasn't about him and his pain, it was about her.

With that thought in mind, he took stock of her with a critical eye. She needed water and food of course, but there was something else that might make her feel even better. He chastised himself for not thinking of it before as he reached in his pocket and pulled out his lip balm, the kind with a high SPF that worked against the sun's punishing rays. Her lips were dry and cracked and must be killing her. He leaned forward and smoothed the balm over her lips which had opened slightly in surprise. When he finished, she beamed at him, as much as she could when smiling too hard could crack her lips wide open.

"Thank you," she whispered. For the first time, he noticed tears shimmering in her eyes. His hand froze, and he braced himself, waiting for her collapse, but it didn't come. After a few determined blinks, the tears were absorbed back into her beautiful ebony eyes.

Truck swallowed hard and looked away as he stuffed his lip balm back in his pocket. How did she do that? And why? In his experience, women were emotional wrecks. They were like ticking time bombs, looking for an excuse to go off. Shelby had the best excuse in the world, and yet she hadn't shed a tear. Why?

And then it hit him, a thought so startling he froze and stared at her again: she was doing it for him. She was reining in her emotions because she didn't want him to have to deal with anything else. In his whole life, no one had ever thought of him, thought how her emotional outburst might affect him. His mother had certainly never taken him into consideration, had never given any thought to the fact that her overly sensitive little son might take every tear to heart and agonize over its presence, might spend hours trying to figure out how to fix her or make her happy. Yet this stranger was doing exactly that. She barely knew him, she was in desperate shape, and she was putting his emotional wellbeing ahead of her own.

Then a new thought struck him, one so startling it trumped all the others that had come before. He was strong enough to handle whatever happened. No longer was he the vulnerable little boy at the mercy of his mother's depression. He was a grown man with the emotional strength and stamina to handle whatever life threw at him, be it gunfire or a woman's tears. He sat up as much as he could in the small enclosure and leaned as close as he dared without frightening her.

"Shelby, you can cry, sweetheart." He rested his free hand on her forehead and swiped it gently over her head, the silk of her hijab smooth under his fingers. For a second as she looked up at him, the pain in her eyes was stark and raw. She seemed to be warring with herself, trying to decide if she was going to give in to her emotions or hold them in check a while longer. After a few seconds of deliberation, she blinked away her pain once more and even managed a grim smile.

"Maybe later," she suggested.

Truck felt oddly disappointed by her refusal. He had worked up the courage to comfort her, and there was nothing to comfort. They were at an impasse now—she refusing to give in to her emotions for fear of burdening him, and him desiring her to give in and stop protecting him.

He settled back against the crusty sand, thinking. Only a few more hours until they arrived at the drop zone. There would be a short flight to Germany, and then he would hand her off to someone else. How would he feel when his task was completed? The problem, he realized was that nothing would feel complete. He would always wonder about her, wonder how she was coping. Somehow she had become more to him than the job, and yet he couldn't seem to muster his usual indignation. There was a reason he didn't like to deal with civilians, and this was it. He translated when he needed to, but otherwise he tried not to interact with the locals because he didn't want to care about them. He was an all or nothing type of person. Either he let someone in completely, or he shut them out completely. There was no middle ground for him.

Each of them coped with the difficulties of their job in their own way—Kelsey by laughing it off and not letting it get to him, Nick by trying to be the perfect leader who made no mistakes, Lolly by praying fervently every chance he got, and Truck by shutting down his emotions completely. That hadn't worked so well with Shelby, but he wasn't falling apart like he feared. He was actively caring for and about someone, and he wasn't losing pieces of his soul as he had with his mother. In fact, it felt a little like he was gaining them back.

He lay back down, puzzling over the new pieces while Shelby fell back asleep.

CHAPTER 7

Shelby didn't feel well. In fact, she felt horrible. This feeling was different from her previous misery. Then she had felt all her aches and pains. Now she felt numb and vague, barely able to hold on to herself, as if her consciousness might slip away without her permission. The feeling scared her. For the first time since the beginning of her ordeal, she began to think she might not make it out alive. On top of all that, it was over a hundred degrees, and she couldn't get warm. She hoped that explained why she woke up shivering, curled into a ball, and pressed into Truck's side. Had she been seeking warmth or comfort? Maybe both.

"Drink this," Truck commanded, sounding severe. With effort she pulled her eyes open and sipped from the water bottle, grimacing as it went down.

"What is that?" she asked. Her voice sounded croaky. The water tasted chalky, sweet, and sour.

"It's water, with some enhancements. It's a tablet that helps balance your electrolytes when you're dehydrated. I always carry them in the desert."

"You shouldn't give that to me," she said. "You should save it for you for when you need it."

He chuckled as he smoothed his hand over her head, making gentle passes over her hijab. "Honey, you're the one who needs it."

The endearment made her smile. It was like being back home. Her eyes remained closed, but she reached out and rested her hand on his chest, then moved it when she encountered his vest. She wanted to touch reassuring flesh, not Kevlar or whatever the military used. Her hand landed on his arm and lingered. "When's the last time you called a woman honey?"

"Not too long. It slips out with Melly occasionally. Now sugar, there's one I haven't used in ages."

"Keep it that way," Shelby commanded. "Sugar is what you call your horse, not a woman."

"What endearment do you prefer, Miss Shelby?" he asked. He took her hand in both his and held it, his thumb surreptitiously checking her pulse.

"Darling," she replied.

His brows knit together. "I'm not sure I can pull that one off."

"That's okay; I was teasing anyway," she said.

"If you're joking, that must be a good sign," he said. His smile didn't reach his eyes because they were filled with worry as he inspected her.

"I don't think I'm up for any marathons today, that's for sure," she said.

"I can carry you the rest of the way," he offered.

The offer was tempting. To not have to plod through the shifting sand on feet that already felt blistered, to be able to conserve the tiny drop of energy she had left. "How far is it?"

"A few more hours."

She blinked at him. She had expected him to say it was a few more feet. "You can't carry me for hours."

"Of course I can," he said. His tone was so matter of fact that she had no doubts he would do it. He had to be nearly as depleted as she. Even lying still in the sweltering sun was enough to drain one's energy and resources. Yet he would carry her for hours through the sand because he made up his mind to do so. His determination encouraged her to keep going on her own—if he could do it, then so could she.

"I'll walk, thank you," she said.

He clucked his tongue. "Stubborn."

She clucked her tongue, exaggerating the sound to imitate him. "Back at you."

"I'm supposed to be stubborn—I'm a marine."

"I'm supposed to be stubborn—I'm a southern female."

"I'm not going to give you any more of my special drink. It's making you sassy," Truck said even as he pulled it out and held the bottle to her lips.

"Honey, I was born sassy," Shelby said, grimacing as she took a sip of the elixir. Maybe it was a placebo effect, but she felt slightly better after each sip of the salty liquid.

"I imagine you were. Scares me that I like it so much. Why can't I find me a woman who's submissive?"

"Because you'd be bored with no one to spar with."

"That's true enough. But for once I'd like to give a woman a command and have her look at me with big doe eyes and say 'Yes, Ashton, whatever you say, Ashton.' Just for the novelty of the experience, mind."

His accent was in full force, and he seemed to be slipping into the vernacular of his youth. Shelby smiled as she watched him drink and resettle their shelter. There was probably some psychological effect going on that made him feel like her new best friend—shared trauma, and all that. Shelby didn't care about the psychology behind the feeling, however; she only cared that she didn't feel so horribly alone for the first time in a long time. Maybe even before the kidnapping. While she had connected with her Saudi family on some level, she had been the American outsider. But now here was Truck who understood and who spoke like everyone else she knew back home. A little of the pressing weight lifted and, for the time being, she felt almost lighthearted, as if nothing bad had happened to her, as if she wasn't stuck in the middle of the desert with a marine for a companion. For now they were simply Ashton and Shelby, and they were friends.

On his side of the tarp, Truck was having similar thoughts. He shouldn't be enjoying what was essentially a dire situation. But as the final hours of the mission wore down, all he could think was that he didn't want it to end, which was selfish. Shelby was in need of medical attention. She should be with her family. But the thought of relinquishing her care and never seeing her again was painful to him. For the first time in a long time, he felt torn by his desire to continue his friendship with her. It occurred to him there was no need to dissect her from his life completely, as if landing in Germany was some magical wormhole that would make her disappear. Technology made the world a small place. She might live far away in Texas, but they could talk on the phone or computer. He was in and out of the country so much it didn't really matter that she wouldn't be at his home base. He barely had a home base. They could do this—they could be friends. He could find closure, he would be able to keep up on her, to know how she was doing.

"Shelby," he began, and then he heard the droning of a plane. This time the sound was more ominous because if they were making a second pass in their search for her, it might mean they had picked up a trail. "Sorry." He apologized in advance as he sprang into action, unfurled the thermal cover, and rolled on top of her. His senses were on high alert as he tried to figure out the meaning of the plane, listening for any signs of advance or retreat. If they didn't clear the area soon, then the combined body heat would begin to seep from under the tarp, giving away their thermal signature. The insulated cover wasn't for the long term—it could only work if the plane was making a quick sweep. Anything longer and they were sitting ducks.

So distracted was he by his thoughts, that it took a long time to notice Shelby's reaction to him—or rather her lack of reaction. She was calm, placid, almost smiling as she lay there chagrined beneath him.

"This is sort of degrading to my modern female sensibilities," she explained in answer to his questioning look. "Having a man throw himself on top of me to protect me sort of does away with the whole notion of being able to look after myself."

"That's ironic because having a handy female to throw myself on and protect goes a long way toward furthering my identity as a marine." She laughed and widened her eyes in surprise as if suddenly realizing she had done so. It was only yesterday she had panicked to the point of hysteria at being this near to a man.

"I guess I've come a long way," she whispered.

"I'm proud of you." There was no reason to whisper, but Truck did it anyway. The moment seemed weighted somehow, an opinion that was furthered when her fingers inched up and brushed his cheek. He closed his eyes and leaned in while she tipped her face up. A rock landed hard on his back and he jumped to attention, as if Nick was giving him a verbal order instead of a physical reminder. Without a doubt it was his commanding officer who had winged him, and with good reason.

As he drew himself back to the present, he realized the plane was gone and the temperature under the cover was about a million degrees. If the plane came back, their thermal stamp would be a glowing red beacon. He threw off the cover and rolled away from her in one fluid motion with a muttered, "Sorry." Sorry for what, he wasn't sure. Sorry for temporarily forgetting he was a marine with a job to do? Sorry for forgetting she was traumatized and shouldn't be kissed now? Sorry for being caught by Nick in such a compromising position? Or sorry because the longed-for kiss hadn't been completed, leaving him frustrated and confused.

"My bad," Shelby muttered, sounding as disoriented as he felt. They glanced at each other, their mutual confusion turning to amusement, and they shared an uncomfortable little laugh.

"Awkward," Truck said.

"Mutually, which sort of cancels out the awkwardness," Shelby said.

And like that the air between them was clear again and they were smiling. Truck was amazed at how easy everything was with her. True, they were insulated from the real world here. But Shelby was different than anyone he had ever known, and he couldn't help but think that difference was what set her apart from the other women in his life. She was charming, if such a moniker could still be applied to someone who was in obvious misery.

"We should eat before we hit the trail again," Truck announced. He pulled out an MRE for each of them, noting as he did so that they had one left. If the chopper was late, they would eat it for breakfast. Hopefully they would have breakfast in Germany. His mouth began to water in anticipation of sausage, so he pushed the thought away. It would do no good to crave sausage while eating MRE's of beef stew, definitely not one of their better offerings.

"I'm so sorry," Shelby said. Her tone was filled with such sincerity that Truck's heart sank. Was she feeling remorse over that accidental almost kiss?

"What for?" he asked, keeping a wary eye on her expression as he handed her the food.

"Because you apparently have to eat these all the time, and they're horrible. If I had any idea the food was this bad, I would have been sending more care packages to soldiers."

"You get used to them, and some are better than others. The desserts are really kind of good, not as good as homemade, of course, but good." He paused, eating. "Do you cook?"

"Let's put it this way: the other members of my family could qualify as gourmet chefs. What do you think?"

"I'll take that as a no," he said. "You could learn."

"What's the point? I'll never be as good as they are," she said.

"That's no way to talk. I wouldn't be here if I had that attitude," Truck said.

"What's that supposed to mean? You're as good as they are, from what I've seen."

"That's because you haven't seen everything. Do you think I could have taken the shot that killed the guy who took you? No, that wasn't me. I only have average aim; I'm not a sniper. Kelsey and Nick are the ones with all the training, and Lolly has some sort of freakish gift for stalking. I basically pull a trigger on a machine gun. I don't even have to aim, I spray whatever's breathing."

"You're being modest. I can tell you're good at what you do, or you wouldn't be here."

"I'm good with languages," Truck said. "That's my gift. I have this uncanny ability to understand languages I've barely ever heard before, and I can speak several fluently. So, see, it wouldn't do anybody any good if I got down on myself because I can't shoot the crosshairs off a hippo from a thousand yards, or can't sneak up on people so they don't know I'm right next to them. I bring my own set of skills to the table."

"The crosshairs off a hippo?" she repeated, quirking an eyebrow.

"Don't make fun of my clever colloquialisms, Miss. And don't change the subject. You've got to stop comparing yourself to your family and find your own thing."

She looked down, staring at her finger as she drew it through the sand. "I thought coming here was my thing. I'm beginning to think I don't have a thing. Maybe I'm the only person in the universe with no talent whatsoever."

"You have a thing, and I can tell you what it is," Ashton said. He paused, waiting for her to look up.

"What is it?" She sounded truly puzzled, and that made him sad. How could she not know the amazing person she was?

"Perseverance," he said.

Her eyebrow quirked again. "That's it? That's my thing? Being able to take a punch and stand up again like a balloon clown?"

"You have no idea what a rare gift that is. I'm serious," he added when she started to laugh. "You might not realize it because you've grown up in a sheltered atmosphere, but the world is hard. Believe me--I see the worst of what humanity has to offer all the time. I deal with the aftermath of tragedy on an almost daily basis. You have no idea how few people keep going, keep putting one foot in front of the other. Most give up. They break, either physically or mentally. Or they turn bitter. But you have been dealing with difficult things your whole life, and you're a sweet and sunny person. That's a gift, Shelby. Don't be ashamed of it, and don't take it for granted."

. . .

"Maybe you're right," she said after a few minutes of thoughtful silence. "Because I think you're the kindest person I've ever met, and if it took this experience for me to meet you, then I can almost believe I'll survive."

"Talk like that will make me blush," he said, and he was only half kidding. People generally commented on his surliness. No one had called him *kind* since he was a kid. It was sort of nice, this partial thawing of his frosty, seldom-used heart.

She lay back, smiling. "Being a graceful failure. That's my thing; I should have known from all the practice I get that I would be a pro by now."

She was being self-deprecating, which was something else he liked about her—she had a solid sense of humor. "Think of how good at failing you'll be by the time you die," he said.

"That's an optimistic thought, Ashton, thank you," she said, patting his hand.

He laughed and gave her hand a squeeze. "C'mon, Shelby from Texas. It's time to mosey for the border."

"You don't say mosey in real life do you?" She sat up and put out her hand when a wave of dizziness assaulted her, belatedly trying to hide it from Truck's inspection.

"In real life I don't say much of anything at all. You're turning me into a blabbermouth. In four years, this is the most my teammates have ever heard me speak."

She froze. "I forgot they can hear us."

"It's okay—this is a safe place."

She looked around at the sand-scarred, snake-infested, scorpion-filled desert. "Figuratively speaking," he added. "The guys don't judge. Well, maybe Kelsey does, but no one pays attention to him anyway." He gave a heads-up nod toward where he thought Kelsey was and was rewarded by a beam of red light centering on his forehead.

Shelby gasped. "Is that a gun scope?"

"No. It's a laser pointer. I told you; he thinks he's hilarious," Truck said.

The light flashed on his forehead a few times, Morse code for "I am." Truck waved him away, and the light disappeared. He put down his hand to help her up, keeping it after she stood.

"They're kind of like your family, huh?"

"Not kind of—they are." He hefted his pack onto his shoulders and clasped her hand again. "I wasn't in good shape when I came to this team. I was well on the road to being an alcoholic. The guys dried me out, gave me a reason to be sober again."

"I don't drink," Shelby volunteered.

"Okay," Truck drawled.

"I said that because I can see now how it would be a kind of coping mechanism for life's little calamities. I guess I'll have to find something else. Maybe food. I could get good and obese if I put my mind to it."

"Please don't," Truck said. "I rather like the look of you now." He didn't need another one of Nick's rocks to his back to let him know the comment had sounded flirtatious, but he hadn't meant it that way. He was being sincere. He hated to see her turn to a self-destructive lifestyle to try and find peace.

"I was kidding. I think. I do love a good cupcake, though. I know the subject of faith is a touchy one for us, but I think that's the only way I'm going to get through this—by buckling down and holding on to what I say I've always believed. I guess you could say this is where the rubber meets the road for me. Do I believe God is good when life is bad? Rationally? Yes. Emotionally? Maybe. I want to, but it's not as easy as I made it sound from the safety of my cushy American life. I think some soul searching is in order when I leave this place."

"I hope you find the faith you're looking for, Shelby," Truck said.

"Ashton, I hope you do, too," she said.

In reply, he tucked his night vision goggles over his eyes and clasped her hand again.

CHAPTER 8

Their progress was slow, alarmingly so, but there was no way Ashton could hurry Shelby along. She was doing the best she could, better than he could have hoped or expected given the amount of pain she was in and her mounting dehydration. He could carry her, but he didn't want to press the issue and upset her. And then he would be more depleted, less able to defend her if they were attacked.

He was becoming edgy about that, too. Before he started going on missions with the team, he would have dismissed intuition as a bunch of bunk, but they had all had gut feelings before something went bad at one time or another. Usually it was Kelsey who suddenly turned serious and antsy. This time it was apparently Truck's turn to get spooked. He tried to tell himself it was because they had the added responsibility of Shelby. Her presence was not only an added burden —though he didn't like to think of her that way anymore—it was also causing a shift in their normal working strategy.

Usually Truck brought up the rear. He was far more comfortable covering the back than being in the middle. Not only because his main objective was to protect their most valuable asset—Nick—but also because he was the one in control. Now he had to trust Nick and

Kelsey to cover all the bases, to be aware of every sound and smell, to not miss anything. If it was only him, he wouldn't be worried. But there was Shelby to think of. What if his team missed something and whoever was out there got close enough to kill Shelby? Or, worse, to not kill her? To take her again and continue their sick game. One thing was for certain: he would die before he let that happen. They would get their hands on her over his dead body and theirs, too.

They were only a few hours from the drop zone, and they were also edging out of the desert—two facts that otherwise would have cheered him. But every step for Shelby was labored. Instead of being relieved, he was alarmed. Their pickup was scheduled for dawn. What should have taken three hours was taking much longer. The sun would be up soon, and they were still too far away. At last Truck made an executive decision.

"Shelby, honey, I'm going to have to carry you the rest of the way. The good news is that it's not too far."

She nodded, expressionless. Truck thought she was too exhausted and sick to care at this point. He picked her up as gently as he could while tossing her over his shoulder in a dead lift, and then he began to jog. While it wasn't exactly a cake walk to run through rocky sandy terrain with someone's weight over one shoulder, it was easier than it had been in training when the person he had been carrying was a two hundred pound marine. Shelby was little more than a hundred pounds and not weighted down by gear. And they were almost there. He only had to run a mile, maybe two at the most before they reached the landing zone.

They arrived and Lolly emerged from the scenery, making Truck realize he had been there the whole time but Truck simply hadn't seen him. He set Shelby down and retrieved water for both of them. He was weaker than he liked to admit. Being in the desert always took too much out of him, and he had been eating and drinking less in order to make sure there was enough for her. Still, he was in much better shape than she was.

She shrank back at the sight of Lolly, and Truck remembered she had been unconscious while Lolly was making his inspection of her.

"This is Lolly," he said, embarrassed by his slight breathlessness. "He's one of ours."

"The one who is good at hiding," Shelby said, though she didn't take a step forward or hold out her hand. She remained shrouded in Truck's shadow, her hands tucked behind her back to stop their obvious trembling.

"Hi," Lolly said. His smile was the only bright spot in his dirt-smudged face, but there was no missing the soft shyness of his words or expression. Usually women were at ease with him because they realized he was harmless, but Shelby simply nodded and maintained her position near Truck.

Nick and Kelsey showed up then. Kelsey was in his rare serious mode, but Truck didn't know if it was because the situation was as dire as he suspected or because he was trying not to frighten Shelby. As it was, the shaking was no longer confined to her hands. Her whole body was trembling as she took a step back and bumped Truck's side. His heart wrenched for her. He knew she didn't want to be afraid of his team, that her irrational reaction was out of her control and she was probably embarrassed by it.

He shifted his gun to his left hand so he could reach out and give her bicep a reassuring squeeze. "The chopper will be here soon. We'll be in Germany before you know it."

She nodded, her black eyes huge with fear, her dark complexion an unhealthy sallow color. Tears shimmered in her eyes. *Not now,* Truck silently pled. *Don't cry now when we're this close to the finish line. Don't fall apart at the end.* She bit her lip and whimpered and he was the one who broke. Shoving his gun at Nick, he wrapped both arms around her and pulled her close so she was resting against his chest, swallowed by his embrace.

Sharp, short breaths wracked her body as she tried to get herself back under control. "It's okay," Truck murmured over and over, smoothing his hand down the back of her hijab. He suddenly hated the thing and wished he could rip it off, but they weren't yet far enough away from the people who demanded its use. If for some reason she was caught without it, she would be severely punished, even in the more progressive country whose border they had just crossed.

Her face was pressed tight to his shirt, but it remained dry. Eventually she somehow pulled herself back under control. The woman had grit; it was only from sheer force of will that she preempted a total breakdown, forcing her tears back to whatever fathomless well they had come from once again. Her breaths became longer, her trembling less violent, but she didn't let go of him. Instead she turned her face to the side and rested her cheek on his chest.

"Sorry," she murmured.

"You're fine," he assured her.

She barked a short, humorless laugh. She was far from fine, and they both knew it.

"Figuratively speaking," he added. He leaned down and pressed a kiss to the top of her scarf, and she smiled, relaxing a little more as she leaned into him.

His teammates pretended to be looking in three different directions, and then he realized they weren't pretending. The sun was fully up now, and there was no chopper. Where was it? He also began scanning the sky, straining his ears for the answering thwack of blades cutting the air, but the air was strangely silent. Too silent. Where were the birds? Where was the wildlife? Were they being followed? Were they being watched?

He turned his attention to Lolly. By now they had spent so much time with each other that words weren't necessary to communicate. They could read each other's body language and expressions and know what was going on, especially in the field. What Truck read in Lolly's body language made him tighten his grip on Shelby. Lolly had a way of shifting into predator mode whenever they were in danger. It was like watching a lion stalk prey as his entire body became still and lethal. He was doing it now as his eyes narrowed on the horizon to their rear. Either they had been followed, or someone had found their trail.

"How far away?" Nick asked Lolly.

"A day behind, but catching up," Lolly replied.

Truck let out his breath. If they were a day behind, then the team and Shelby would be long gone by the time whoever was tracking them caught up. Unless they weren't, unless that was why Lolly and Nick were now sharing *the look*, the things-are-about-to-get-really-bad look.

Nick cleared his throat, trying to say things gently and in code for Shelby's sake. "I don't think the chopper is coming right now. We're going to have to get to a radio."

A lot of words went through Truck's mind then, and none of them would he say in front of the delicate female in his arms. There was a radio in the next town, a few more hours away by foot. But they didn't know exactly where; they only knew that a mole sometimes managed to contact someone to pass information along. Not only would they have to hike another day, but they were being followed.

"We'll take turns carrying the girl," Kelsey said. His expression was grim for once. As much as Kelsey sometimes got on his nerves, Truck would rather see him annoyingly cheerful over this wary, nervous look.

"No," Shelby said. Her hands formed claws that clung to Truck's vest. "I can make it. I'll walk—I'll try to walk fast."

Everyone but Shelby looked at Nick. She didn't realize it, but she didn't have the final say here—Nick did. He nodded once. "As long as we can keep a good pace," he added. Then, addressing Shelby. "I don't want to pressure you to push yourself beyond your means, but we need to make quick time. If for some reason we're not going fast enough, then we're going to have to take turns carrying you."

"I understand. If that's what it comes down to, then so be it. But I'd like to try and walk if I can."

Now it was Nick's turn to nod. "Ready?" he asked her.

She nodded, not looking at all certain, and they were off again. Truck felt like a mother hen. Nick still had his gun. On a normal mission, he felt like a piece of his arm was missing if he didn't have it on him at all times, but now he couldn't seem to focus on anything but Shelby. She was already functioning on fumes. Where would she find the resolve to keep putting one foot in front of the other?

"Why wasn't the helicopter there?" she asked.

"There's a lot of political unrest in this area," Truck said. "It could be that its presence was detected so near the border. This isn't exactly a unique situation. Since we're so far off the radar, our plans have to be fluid. You learn to go with the flow and take things in stride." Something much easier to accomplish when they didn't have an injured, untrained woman in their midst.

"Maybe I should join the marines when this is over," Shelby suggested, the faint humor back in her tone.

"You'd have to learn to like MRE's," Truck reminded her.

"That settles it, then. The military is not for me. Too bad—I was this close to joining up." She held her hand aloft, fingers together. "Y'all are showing me such a good time, I was momentarily duped into believing this was the life for me. To think you get to trudge through the sand without food or water whenever you want."

"Don't forget the cruddy pay and no time off," Truck added. "Or perks, as we like to call them."

"Now you're teasing me with what I can't have," Shelby said. "The fast food industry is going to seem like paradise after this."

"Really?" Truck said.

"No. Nothing could ever make that happen. But at least they have air conditioning."

"Don't go back to that life, Shelby. You were meant for bigger things," Truck said.

"It's hard to believe that when I can barely write my own name without getting the letters mixed up," Shelby said.

"You'll find your niche. Not all jobs require book smarts. This one, for instance. It might surprise you to know I was not valedictorian of my class."

She was quiet for a while after that, whether processing their conversation or conserving energy he didn't know. They were out of the desert, but it was still sweltering. They were all being quiet, but Lolly, Nick, and Kelsey were more guarded than thoughtful. Shelby was making good time, better than they could have hoped. But if they were without her, they would have run. The slow progress was nerve-wracking because it meant whoever was following was gaining on them.

The silence became tenser and heavier as the day proceeded, for all except Shelby. Her silence was born of conservation. She failed to think, failed to feel, and continued only to function, putting maximum effort into placing one foot in front of the other. For a while she amused herself by imagining a spa day when she returned home. She would have her hair washed and conditioned. She would get a facial, pedicure, and massage. Then the last ounce of her energy fled, and she had no imagination left. Her mind was a blank, dark canvass with no pictures or words. All she knew was that if she stopped, she would never start again.

That was why when Truck suggested stopping for lunch and water, she refused. Instead, she held out her hand for an MRE and kept walking while she ate. The food was tasteless, the water burned her throat, but still she kept trudging along. At last they came to a house of sorts. The main portion was a round straw yurt that had been added onto with whatever materials were handy—one part was adobe-style clay while the other was cinder block. There was a camel keeping watch in the front yard. At any other time, Shelby would have been intrigued by the haphazard styles and what she could only assume was a guard camel, but her brain was too numb.

The men in her party were not numb, however, and since this was the first habitat they reached after leaving the desert, they were on high alert.

"Why can't they make it easy and hang out the 'I'm a bad guy' flag for us?" Kelsey whispered. "That way we would know if we have to do this the hard way or the easy way."

"What do we have to do?" Shelby whispered. Her throat was croaky and sore, and so were her lips. Ashton frowned as he pulled out his lip balm and smoothed it over her mouth.

"We need to go in," he said. "We're out of provisions."

Somehow Shelby knew that if she wasn't with them, then they wouldn't go in. They would bypass the strange-looking abode, go straight to wherever the radio was, and get out of the country. But it was obvious she was on her last legs and in desperate need of rest, food, and water. Not that they were guaranteed to find any of those things here. She guessed no one lived this close to the desert and far from town without good purpose, and often those who were secluded chose to be so for a reason.

A face popped into one of the greasy-looking windows. "Holy chiminea," Kelsey said, obviously editing himself when he glanced at Shelby. "Where did she come from?"

The woman had a broad, dark face, pruned from too many years in the sun. She resembled a Russian babushka, only she was wearing a hijab and not a loosely-tied scarf, alerting Shelby to the fact that— wherever they were—they were still in conservative Muslim territory.

"I guess killing her is out," Kelsey murmured. "She looks like my grandma."

"Truck, Lolly, you're up," Nick said. "We'll hang back and cover you."

Truck stared at the house, his head tipped as he decided on his approach. "I'll need to take Shelby with me." He put his arm around her and drew her against his side. "Don't say a word in there," he told her. "Just stand still and look pathetic."

"Done and done," Shelby whispered. At this point she wasn't sure if she could walk to the door. Ashton must have guessed as much because he cinched his arm around her and practically carried her forward. She stood between him and the little one called Lolly who stuck out his hand and knocked on the door. Shelby almost did a double take when she glanced at his face. Gone was the hard-bodied marine and in his place was a doe-eyed innocent. He looked completely harmless and no older than fifteen. As she watched, he bit his lip hard enough to draw tears so when the woman opened the door his already large black eyes were shimmering.

The woman opened the door, which was sort of amazing. If Shelby lived in the middle of nowhere and four heavily-armed, burly marines and a bedraggled woman came knocking, there is nothing that would compel her to answer.

She spoke in Arabic, scanning their faces as she took in the scene before her. Ashton answered her in a fluent stream of Arabic, gesturing to Shelby and his companions occasionally. Shelby had no idea what he was saying but he sounded plaintive. She remembered what he told her and tried to look pathetic; it didn't take a lot of acting on her part. The woman smiled, nodding, as she backed up and made room for them to enter. Lolly went first, and then Ashton helped Shelby through the door. Nick and Kelsey stayed outside, presumably to keep watch. The woman could very well be a prop; armed insurgents could be anywhere in these parts, a fact Shelby was learning the hard way. The constant fear was almost becoming second nature so that instead of a flooding rush of adrenaline, there was a small, continual stream that kept the senses on constant high alert. *The guys must crash when they finally get home,* Shelby thought. Being mentally "on" all the time was exhausting.

The house was sweltering and redolent with the scent of meat and spices. There was a fire pit in the center of the yurt portion—its flames leaping high and licking at a few kabobs of meat splayed over a grate. The heat, the smell, the fear, and her own weakness rose up to smack Shelby in the face. She needed to inform Truck that she had hit the proverbial wall, but he and the old woman were talking like new best friends. All the while the room began to pitch and spin, her vision faded in and out, and a loud ringing sounded in her ears.

I think I'm going to faint, she said, or at least that's what she thought she said. In reality she opened her mouth, closed her eyes, and sank to the floor.

CHAPTER 9

Truck caught her before her head hit the dirt. Scooping her up, he turned helplessly toward the woman, hoping she would offer some of the hospitality the locals were known for; she didn't disappoint.

"Bring her here," she said, although she said it in Arabic, so Truck had to translate for Lolly who remained guardedly in the living room. He had a good feeling about the woman, but feelings had been wrong before. They would continue to observe all the necessary precautions while they were here, which meant Nick and Kelsey were stuck outside for the duration. But he had said the magic words—American money—and there was now nothing too good for the woman's new favorite people. Her husband worked as a camel broker—offering up camels to whoever was unlucky enough to need one before plunging into the desert. Since there weren't a lot of tourists hoping to cross into hostile territory, they probably barely eked out a living. They could survive for a year or more on what Nick would pay them for their kindness, but sometimes not even the promise of a lot of money could buy loyalty. So they would wait here until Shelby recovered, but they wouldn't let down their guards because complacency could get them killed.

The woman motioned to a mattress on the floor. It wasn't clean by hospital standards, but Truck had seen much worse. He had the sense the woman did the best with what she had to work with, and he complimented her on her tidy, cozy house. She beamed at him, a toothless grin with a hint of a girlish blush, and he smiled in return. He hoped he wasn't wrong about her and she was as sweet and innocent as she seemed. It would be a real pain to have to kill her. She said something else and he nodded his assent, waiting until she was out of the room before he sank to his knees beside the bed.

"Now is the time to wake up, Shelby. C'mon, honey. Please, please, please, you've got to wake up here, or things are about to get really awkward. Baby, please." He spoke in furious whispers, finishing long before the woman returned. It was hopeless; Shelby was out cold.

The lady returned, a large bowl of hot water and clean rags in her hand.

"What's your name?" Truck asked. She was fluent in Arabic, although her first language was Russian. His Arabic was better, and that's what they used to communicate.

"Dursun," she replied. "Shall I wash her for you?" She indicated the bowl and rags.

Truck sighed. "No, I'll do it." When he made up their cover story, he had been proud of himself for coming up with something that would ensure he was by Shelby's side at all times. Now he was filled with regret because he was stuck. He couldn't leave Dursun alone with Shelby because he didn't trust her. He couldn't stand back and let her do the washing because she would discover the nature of Shelby's injury and either guess that his story was a lie or think Truck was the one who had assaulted her. That left him option C: wash Shelby himself.

He tried not to look nervous as Dursun handed him the supplies, but he must not have succeeded because she lingered. "Do you need anything else?"

"No, thank you. This will do."

"I'll make her a special brew, something that will help her feel better."

"Thank you." He would have Lolly watch every step of that brew to make sure it wasn't poisoned, intentionally or accidentally. The water here wasn't exactly potable, at least not for outsiders who hadn't built up a tolerance to the native parasites. "Thank you, Dursun. Your hospitality becomes you." They were in Turkmenistan now, a country well-known for hospitality. To not comment on it would be rude. The problem was that they were so near the border of a not-so-hospitable country that one could never be sure of allegiances. The country's official position was one of neutrality. Its citizens, however, did not always adhere.

She scuttled out of the room, leaving Truck alone with Shelby and the bowl of water. Now what? If he didn't clean Shelby, then Dursun might find it odd and get suspicious. But if he did, wasn't it one more invasion of her already shattered privacy? She had to be uncomfortable, though. Washing her would undoubtedly make her feel better.

He was tempted to call Lolly and hand the job to him. As their resident medical expert, Lolly had become pretty good at viewing such tasks as an innocuous part of the job. But chances were good Lolly had never seen a naked woman before, and Truck didn't want Shelby to be the first. And deep down he knew that if someone had to do it, she would want him to be the one. He squinched his eyes closed and took a deep breath, not sure he had ever dreaded touching a pretty woman more than he did at this moment.

"I hope you can forgive me for this," he whispered. Then he dunked the rag in the water and set to work, starting on her forehead in the hopes she might wake and tell him to go away.

* * *

When Shelby woke, she realized something was different—namely that her underpants were missing. Panic overwhelmed her and she sat up, dazed. Had she been kidnapped again? But, no, Truck was sitting beside the bed, his head drooping with sleep. His slumber must have been light because at the slightest sound from her he startled awake.

"You're safe," he told her, guessing her panic by the pale, pinched look of her features.

"What happened to my underwear?" she blurted.

He winced. "I was hoping it would take you longer to notice that. Lie down." He reached out to push her back against the lumpy mattress. Whatever it was made of, it wasn't comfortable. Though Truck was the most likely culprit in her missing undergarments, so complete was her trust in him that she felt more curiosity than alarm. He must have had a good reason. "Put your feet up," he added. "Lolly says it will help with the bleeding."

There was a wad of rolled rags at her feet. She propped her feet on them. The pinching in her hips told her she had probably been in that position for a long time before she woke up and moved. "How long was I out?"

"Five hours."

"I'm sorry," she said, automatically knowing that any delay was putting them in greater danger.

"It's okay. We're taking care of it."

"What does that mean?"

"It means Kelse and Lolly are setting a false trail to lead them away from here. When they're sure it's working, they'll double back and return for us."

"And if it doesn't work? If they find us here?"

"Then Nick and I will handle it," Truck replied. His tone was mild, but the steel in his eyes promised violence, almost as if he was looking forward to the chance to take out whoever was following them. Since they were most likely the people who had kidnapped Shelby, she couldn't really blame him. She hadn't yet reached the soft-hearted forgiveness stage of healing yet; she still felt a fair amount of bloodlust and hatred for her captors. Someday she would have to forgive them. Not now. Right now she needed all the anger she could muster to fuel her steps and keep her from falling apart.

"My underwear..." she prompted.

Ashton bit his lip and took her hand, looking for the first time uncertain. He dropped his voice to a whisper. "I had to think of something to tell her so I would be allowed to stay with you. The moral code in this part of the world is high. No way would they let an unmarried man and woman share a sleeping space. So I told her we're married. You were raised in the US, came back to see your father who demanded a dowry for you. I paid the dowry and we were married, but he still wouldn't give you to me, so I brought back some of my friends and we sneaked you out of the country. I also told her you suffered a miscarriage during our escape, and that's what all the blood was from."

"You really covered all the bases," she said.

"I've gotten pretty good at lying to the locals. We've had to manipulate a lot of innocent people; I try to do it in the best way possible, and then leave them a lot of money to ease my conscience."

"And my underwear…" she reminded him.

He sighed. "Not going to let that go, huh? She offered to clean you. I couldn't let her because then she would see the truth of your injuries and either know I had lied to her or think I was the one who hurt you. So I did it myself."

His tone was straightforward, but he ruined the effect by dropping his eyes and blushing. Shelby was fairly certain it was the first time he had blushed in his adult life, and if it had been any other situation, she would have laughed. Who knew plain-spoken and straightforward Truck had a blush in him? Instead of finding amusement in his blush, she worked up one of her own. "You washed me?" she said the words slowly, embarrassment and shame flooding her with every breath.

"It wasn't as bad as you think," Truck said. "I washed the blood off your legs. I closed my eyes when I took off your underwear. I didn't see anything more than the tops of your legs, nothing more than I would see if you were wearing shorts. I promise—there was no peeking. Your underwear is unsalvageable, by the way. Dursun was going to try and wash it, but we had to throw it out." He didn't mention that the garment, as well as her legs, were crusted in layers of blood. It was a wonder she was still standing with such a monumental blood loss. He hoped she was slightly more comfortable, but he doubted it. To have lost so much blood, she must be in horrible pain.

Shelby was quiet, still not sure how she felt about the situation. He was right—it wasn't as bad as she thought. But it was still humbling and intimate to be washed by someone. It could have been worse, though. It could have been done by someone else. If someone had to do it, she was glad it was him.

"Hey," Truck said, picking up her hand. His voice was soft and warm, his accent in full force. "It's possible that by saying we're married in such a remote place we actually are married now. Who knows what their laws are on that sort of thing? And if a husband can't take proper care of his wife, then I don't want to believe in marriage anymore." He offered up a tentative smile, and she took it, allowing it to soothe her. The heat slowly left her red cheeks as he smoothed his free hand over her head.

"I wish I could take a real bath," she murmured. Even though she had slept for hours, she felt drowsy again. "It might surprise you to know that I usually smell good."

"It might surprise you to know the same about me, but we're safer if we're not covered in perfume. A bath will have to wait. Besides, even covered in dirt and sand you're about the prettiest lady I've ever set my eyes on."

That was definitely worth opening her eyes for, and when she looked at him he was smiling and he looked *sincere*. How could he think she was pretty when she looked like this? With a shower, hair products, makeup, and a nice dress she could look pretty good. But her head was covered in a grimy hijab, she hadn't bathed in a month, to say nothing of her stained and smelly robe. "I think the desert sun has affected your mind, Ashton," she said. She pressed her palm to his cheek, noting its smoothness. "Did you shave?"

"No, ma'am. You have stumbled on to my deep, dark and humiliating secret: I can't grow facial hair. Don't tell the others. They think I shave every few hours to keep up my clean-cut appearance." He winked, letting her know he was teasing. Of course his teammates would know he couldn't shave in the middle of the desert, but she liked the conspiratorial feeling it gave her to think they were keeping a secret together.

She made an X over her heart. "Cross my heart. Our little secret."

"That's my girl," Truck said. When the old woman, Dursun, entered, they probably did look like a newlywed couple, their heads bent close together as they whispered and smiled. She spoke to Truck and he nodded, transferring his smile to her. She handed him a mug, and he took it. Shelby knew about four phrases of Arabic, and she recognized when he said "Thank you."

"Thank you," she added to Dursun. Might as well expend all the phrases she knew while she was here, especially because she was thankful. It wasn't everyone who would give up her bed to a bleeding stranger, American money or not.

Dursun bestowed a compassionate smile on her and unleashed a stream of words Shelby had no hope of understanding. She smiled nonetheless and turned to Ashton when Dursun left the room.

"She said she miscarried early in her marriage, too, and went on to have several babies. She said not to worry—you're young and healthy and there will be more children in your future," he translated, staring down into the mug as he spoke.

Shelby drew in a sharp breath. Would there be children in her future? Was the damage irreparable? And what if she was pregnant? For the last two years, she had been taking birth control for her irregular cycles. But she hadn't taken any pills once she was kidnapped. And she had been assaulted daily during most of that time, sometimes more than once a day. Was that what the blood was from? Had she actually had a miscarriage?

"Shelby, drink, honey," Truck commanded. His velvety voice jerked her back to the present. He helped her to sit up and held the cup for her as she sipped. The brew was bitter and metallic. She grimaced even though she drank greedily. Apparently being parched could compel one to drink even the most disgusting tonic.

"What is it?" she asked when she had drained the mug.

"Some herbal concoction. Lolly said it's safe. She boiled it for a while, but I still added an iodine tablet. That probably accounts for some of the bad taste. You can't be too careful with the water here. Don't drink anything without checking with me first."

She drank mindlessly and soon realized she had drained the whole thing without offering any to him. "I'm so sorry," she said. She rested her hand on his arm. "I'm a selfish pig. I should have shared that."

"Dursun made it specifically for, uh, female problems. It's probably better I didn't have any. Might get me in touch with my feminine side, and the world as we know it would collapse." She still looked troubled, so he jostled her hand. "I'm teasing, honey. I ate and drank already. Dursun makes a mean goat kabob."

"Goat?" Shelby asked. At any other time she might have been put off by the idea of eating goat kabobs cooked in a yurt in the middle of nowhere. Now it sounded like the best thing she had ever heard of. "What does goat taste like?"

"Have you ever smelled a goat?" Ashton asked. "That's what goat tastes like. But she adds a bunch of spices to it, and it's really delicious."

As if she knew they were talking about her food, Dursun brought a plate of goat and a bowl of yogurt made from camel's milk. She said something to Truck as she set it down. He smiled and thanked her again, so Shelby did the same. Dursun nodded, smiling, as she backed out of the room.

"She said camel's milk is especially healthy. It has curative properties that will help with whatever is wrong with you. And she said they have plenty because their camel recently calved, so you can have as much as you want."

Shelby tasted the food and found it as delicious as Truck had said it would be. The goat meat was slightly gamey and a little greasy, but the spices were a wonderful complement, and she was too ravenous to be picky. The camel-milk yogurt was runnier than yogurt she was used to, but it was sweet and tangy—the perfect complement to the meat. She had almost finished everything when she remembered Truck was still sitting beside her. She paused with the spoon halfway to her mouth and gave him a guilty, caught look. "Want some?" she asked.

He shook his head.

"Try some of this yogurt," she urged, holding out her spoon for him. He took the bite and shrugged.

"It's yogurt. I don't get women and their love of yogurt."

"It's comforting, I guess."

"A steak and cold beer, now that's comforting," Truck replied.

Shelby wrinkled her nose. "How can you drink that stuff? It smells like feet."

"It tastes like feet," he agreed. "But it goes down cold and works wonders after a long, stressful day."

She couldn't really chastise him for using alcohol as a stress reliever when she did the same thing with chocolate. Especially brownies—she had a thing with those. "I haven't had a brownie in months," she blurted, blatant longing in her tone.

"We'll get you one in Germany," Truck promised. "They don't make them the same as we do, but they're still good. And if we can get our hands on some Belgian chocolate, then you'll forget about America completely."

"You like chocolate?" she asked.

"It's a well-known fact that I have a sweet tooth the size of Rhode Island," he said. "Chocolate has its merits, but fruit pie and cobbler, those are my real weakness."

"Watch out, Ashton, I make a mean apple pie."

"Don't tease me, now," he said.

"I'll make one for you," she promised. Her smile slipped. "Sometime, I suppose." Maybe she could ship one from Texas to North Carolina.

"You'll make me one, and I'll grill you a steak. We'll eat on my patio —which is basically a square of concrete, but it has a nice view of the neighbor's wisteria. And after we eat our steak and pie, I'll take you to the ocean and we'll walk on the beach, just the two of us. Have you ever been to the Atlantic?"

"Only the Gulf of Mexico." She bit her lip and sat back as he took her tray and set it aside. He picked up her hand and held it between both of his as he continued his fairytale narrative.

"I'll introduce you to Melly and Ashleigh. You three will hit it off right away. Y'all are peas in a pod—take my word for it. We'll have a party with the girls and Caleigh, that's Ashleigh's little sister and the object of Lolly's affection. Everyone will pair up and make out like it's high school all over again. We'll dim the lights and sit on the couch together, clean and well fed and together. We'll be together."

"You sure do paint a pretty picture, Ashton Rucker," Shelby said. In his version of events, she wasn't dealing with the after effects of her assault. He made her sound normal and happy, and she closed her eyes, imagining that it was so. He rubbed his cheek on her palm.

"It'll be okay, Shelby. You'll see," he promised.

She smiled and, for a moment, allowed herself to believe him.

CHAPTER 10

"How's the patient?"

Nick, the team leader, hovered in the doorway. Ashton was tall, but Nick was taller and broader. Beneath the edge of one sleeve Shelby caught sight of a tattoo, but despite his tattoos and size, he had a kind face. Or so she told herself. Her natural reaction to all men was now immediate fear and panic, something that had never happened to her before.

"I'm okay," she said. She sounded shy and uncertain, which was another oddity because she was usually extroverted and talkative.

He smiled, and she gave one in return, though hers was probably tremulous at best.

"It's my turn on watch," Ashton said. He squeezed her hand and stood. "I'll be back in a few hours. Do you need anything else?"

She shook her head, still eying Nick. If Ashton was on watch, then it was Nick's turn to rest. Where would he go? There were no other rooms beside the fire-laden yurt and this addition, whatever it was. There was another addition to the house, but it appeared to be some type of equipment storage, possibly saddles for the camels. Certainly no place for a sleepy soldier. But as Ashton started to leave, Nick backed out, too.

"Wait," she made herself call. "You can sleep in here." There was no sincerity in her tone because she didn't mean it. She didn't want him in the room with her; she was terrified of him. But her rational mind told her she was safe. He was Ashton's friend and team leader. He wouldn't hurt her, and he needed a comfortable place to sleep.

"I can sleep outside," Nick said. He had a pleasant smile. She made herself focus on that as she answered.

"No, please. There's plenty of room in here." She felt a little panicked as she realized he might think she was offering to share the bed. Surely he wouldn't think that, would he? Her heart started to thrum wildly in her chest as he ducked into the room.

"Thank you," he said. He set down his gear on the far side of the room, if such a tiny space could be called far, and Shelby forced herself to relax. Of course he didn't think she was offering to share the small bed. He was an engaged man and she was disgusting. The fact that Ashton could stand to be around her bore testament to his strong stomach. She smelled like blood and sweat and probably looked even worse.

She glanced away from Nick, embarrassment temporarily over-riding her fear. Nick was a handsome man. Unlike Ashton's smooth cheeks, Nick's were stubbly with a thick growth of beard. His hair and eyes were brown, his nose slightly crooked, but in a roguish sort of way that made you believe he was a soft-hearted teddy bear. Shelby was used to men looking at her in a way that let her know she was attractive. Even though she didn't date often, she enjoyed those looks. Or she used to. Nick certainly wasn't looking at her like that. He was looking at her with sympathy or—worse—pity. It was how all men would look at her from now on. Story of her capture and probable death had no doubt made national headlines, as would news of her rescue and return. There was no way the truth wouldn't leak out. The entire country would know what had happened to her. She would never be able to go anywhere again without men giving her the look, the I-know-what-happened-to-you-and-I'm-so-sorry look.

An old-fashioned term popped into her head and lingered. *Soiled dove.* That's what she was now. Through no fault of her own, her innocence had been stripped away, and she was forever altered. No one would ever look at her without remembering what had happened to her, putting themselves in her shoes, wondering how she felt, how she was coping.

"Ashton tells me you're engaged," she said. He no doubt wanted to sleep, but she was desperate for a distraction and a way to tamp down her mounting fear. She had grown used to Ashton's scent; Nick's body odor was making her panic meter ping off the charts again.

"To Ashleigh," Nick confirmed. "Would you like to see a picture?"

"Sure," Shelby replied, delighted by such a normal conversation. Nick reached in his shirt. She didn't think it was an accident that he withdrew the picture from the pocket over his heart, glancing at it with a smile before he handed it to her.

She wasn't sure what she expected Ashleigh to look like, but she was surprised by what she found. She looked so normal, like any one of Shelby's friends back in Texas. Her hair was long and dark brown, her nose dotted by an array of freckles. Shelby found them adorable, but she would guess Ashleigh hated them—most women did. In the picture, she and Nick were standing together, smiling and obviously very much in love.

"She looks sweet," Shelby said.

"She is. And also the most stubborn woman on the planet. Drives me crazy and keeps me hopping." He reached for the picture when she held it out. Their fingers brushed and Shelby jerked her hand back. If Nick noticed, he pretended not to. "I miss her," he added. "And it's only going to get worse. I'm going to Officer Candidate School as soon as we return. Wish me luck I can convince Ashleigh to marry me as soon as it's over. She has some crazy notion that weddings take a lot of planning. Women." He rolled his eyes and lay back down.

Shelby smiled. Either he was making an effort to be especially kind, or he was a naturally sensitive person. Whatever the reason, she appreciated it. It was difficult to be afraid of someone who was working so hard to make sure you weren't.

He closed his eyes. She thought he was asleep until he spoke again. "Ashleigh was abused," he said, his voice barely above a whisper. "I don't think she would mind me sharing that with you; she's fairly open about it. Her ex-boyfriend beat her a few times. She didn't think she would ever date anyone after that, then she fell for me—a sniper who looks like the leader of a biker gang. Sometimes even now when I stretch she flinches away from me, and we laugh because of course I would never hurt her. But those old instincts and feelings take a while to fade." He paused again, and the rest of his words edged out, haltingly, as if he wasn't quite comfortable talking about such things. "Her faith is huge. She's loaned some of it to me, and it's changed me from a desperado to a guy who can't wait to be tied down by kids. I couldn't help but overhear your conversations with Truck. I know Ashleigh's story isn't like yours, but I thought you should know that even though things seem dark right now, time has a way of healing." He yawned, closed his eyes, and a second later he was softly snoring.

Meanwhile Shelby lay back and stared at the ceiling. Sleep was restorative; she should get as much of it as possible while she was here, but Nick's nearness made that impossible. The rational part of her brain trusted him and knew he wouldn't harm her. The emotional part was jumpy and skittish, straining her ears for his even breathing so she would know the minute he woke up.

His words about his fiancée played over and over in her head. The woman in the picture looked whole and healthy, certainly not like someone who had been in an abusive relationship. The old optimistic Shelby wanted to take comfort in that fact and hope that healing was in her future. The newly formed pessimistic Shelby pointed out the vast differences in their stories. Still, pain was pain, wasn't it? Who was to say her pain trumped Ashleigh's because she was the one experiencing it? She argued with herself for the duration of Nick's rest.

Time heals all wounds.

Even this?

God has a plan.

Why would such horror ever be part of God's plan?

Over and over her mind ran while Nick slept and the day turned into night.

"Hey, Darlin.'"

Nick came to with a start and looked at Ashton in the doorway. Without a word, he rolled to his feet and left the room to take his turn at watch.

"Hey," Shelby said.

Ashton came into the room and knelt beside her. "How did that sound? Did I pull off darlin' okay? Because I could add it to my repertoire."

"It didn't work for me. When I said I wanted to be called darling, I was going for more of a Mr. Darcy 'You are my one and only darling' type of thing. Yours was more of a John Wayne lil' darlin' type of endearment. Thanks for trying, though." She patted his hand and he grasped it, bringing it to his lips.

"Mr. Darcy. That's the type of stuff you're into? What is it with women and that guy?"

"He's dreamy. At first he's surly, then you realize how much he loves Elizabeth, how totally devoted he is."

"Surly with a heart of gold. If only there was someone in real life like that." He tapped his chest and Shelby laughed.

"Yes, but you're lacking a castle and British accent. I forgot to mention those before."

"You don't know that I don't own a castle, and I am excellent with British accents. 'Ello guvna." He affected a deep cockney accent, and she laughed harder. He had to be exhausted after four hours standing watch, but he was purposely trying to cheer her up.

"My apologies. You are Mr. Darcy in camo. Don't know how I didn't see it before."

"I would reply and tell you you're like the main character of whatever story he's from, but I am still fully in control of my man card and therefore have no idea what movie we're talking about."

"*Pride and Prejudice,* and here's a tip for you: Unless you want that man card to die alone, I suggest you read the book. It took me six grueling months to dyslexia my way through it, but it was worth it."

"Duly noted." He yawned, triggering a reciprocal yawn in Shelby.

"Go to sleep," she suggested.

"I will. I'm tuckered." He stood and edged away, preparing to take over Nick's spot on the floor.

"You could sleep here. If you want." She gave the lumpy bed a half-hearted pat. "It's not incredibly comfortable, but anything is better than the floor."

He froze, his multi-functioning belt in his hand. "That would be okay with you?"

"It would be okay," she said. She bit her lip, feeling shy. She had become so used to his nearness that having him beside her would feel like blessed relief. Then it occurred to her that he might not want to sleep near her. She didn't exactly smell or look like a rose right now. "Unless you don't want…" she didn't get to finish before he was beside her.

"Less talking, more sleeping," he said. His arm slung over her waist and he froze again, his eyes popping open. Apparently the action had been a reflex, and now he was regretting it. Or maybe he was simply afraid he had frightened her. He hadn't, but how best to make him understand?

She turned toward him, nestling closer. Tentatively, slowly, his arm curved around her back, holding her close, sheltering her. Her hand rested against his chest, but there was no answering warmth through the Kevlar or whatever his vest was called. For Shelby, who had craved comfort and security since the beginning of her ordeal, the feeling of being in his arms was like a little taste of heaven. He was warm, solid, and there. He was one of the good guys, and she was *safe*.

Her hand fisted around his shirt. Curling it toward her like a baby holding a security blanket, she let out a sigh she might have been holding for weeks.

"Sleep, Shelby," he whispered, and she did.

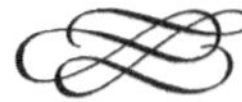

CHAPTER 11

"This is cozy."

Shelby's eyes flapped open. Truck's other arm was around her now, and her head was pillowed on his bicep. The voice was coming from the doorway and panic slammed through her midsection. She started to jump and flinch away, but Ashton stilled her.

"It's Kelsey." Frowning toward the doorway he added, "You scared her."

"Sorry," Kelsey said, looking and sounding contrite. "I came to tell you we're back. You're taking the baby to go for the radio."

"The baby?" Shelby repeated, glancing questioningly at Ashton.

"Lolly. Are you watching or sleeping?" he asked Kelsey.

"Sleeping. I've been up since 1999. Whit's doubling up on watch." As if to emphasize how tired he was, he yawned and stretched, filling the small doorway. He was as large as Nick, though more innocent and boyish looking. His hair was sandy blond and his eyes were a startling shade of blue-green. He had the look of someone who would be at home with a boogie board on a beach somewhere. Or on a Hollywood movie set. He was dazzlingly, befuddlingly handsome, or he would have been if Shelby was her normal self. As it was all she felt was her usual measure of alarm over his presence.

She tried and failed to hide her fear from Ashton. "You're leaving?" She thought that was what Kelsey was trying to say, but her brain felt dull and Kelsey had a way of saying everything so it sounded like a joke. His friends apparently knew how to tell what was serious and what wasn't, but Shelby didn't.

He stood and attached his gear. "I'm leaving, but I'll be back as soon as I can. Do you want Kelse to stay in here with you or leave you alone?"

"You're sleeping, right?" she asked Kelsey. He nodded. "You can stay. Over there." She pointed to the far corner. He turned around to hide his smile.

"You don't know him well enough to realize, but his head is about to explode with stifled commentary right now," Ashton said. He leaned in cupping her face in his hands. "You need anything ask Nick or Kelsey. If they can't get it for you, then Dursun will. Sleep and I'll try to be back when you wake up." He kissed her, a gentle press of his lips to hers, somewhere between romance and affection. She was too stunned to respond. Instead she blinked and nodded stupidly.

"Be safe," she said, finally conjuring her voice. "Is that the right thing to say?"

"That works fine." He chucked her under the chin and, combined with his reassuring smile, Shelby suddenly felt six years old.

"I'll be fine," she assured him, infusing her voice with some reserve of inner steel. He looked more reassured as he left the room. Her gaze fell on Kelsey who was watching her with an amused smile.

"What?" she asked.

He shook his head. "Life never ceases to amaze me, y'know? All the women in the world and Truck falls for someone while on a mission. It's funny." Then, realizing he had once again said something insensitive, he tried to backpedal. "I mean, not that this situation is funny. It's just..."

She took pity on them both by interrupting. "You know what's funny? I'm trapped in a bedroom in the middle of nowhere with a gorgeous marine, and all I want to do is sleep."

He chuckled. "Kudos to you for noting my extreme good looks. More and more the women who surround this team try to see me as more than a pretty face when I am absolutely not. It's nice to be appreciated by someone shallow once in a while."

Shelby snickered. "I don't see any depth at all. As far as I'm concerned, you don't even have to talk. Lie there and look beautiful, man candy."

"You are speaking my language, Shelby Whatever-your-last-name-is. See? I didn't bother to learn it. That's how deep I am, and proud of it. Arm decor, that's me. Someday I'll find a cougar who appreciates me for me, a sugar mama to set me up real nice. Then I can get out of this outfit and lie near a pool doing nothing but doling out compliments on my lady's most recent plastic surgery. 'You had another face lift, Deborah? I didn't notice. But, baby, why do your lips meet in the back of your head when you smile now?'"

Shelby guffawed and then groaned as she realized her bladder was suddenly near bursting. "Oh, I don't suppose this place has indoor plumbing."

"If by indoor plumbing you mean a bowl of what I can only hope is water sitting by the door, then yes, yes it does," Kelsey said.

She laughed and groaned again, hunching over. "Where should I go?"

"There's an outhouse in the back." He rolled off his pallet. "C'mon, I'll take you."

She bit her lip and blinked up at him, eyes suddenly wide and full of fear. It was one thing to banter with him while he was safely across the room and another to see all six foot three of him looming over her.

"It's okay," he soothed, his joking tone set aside for the moment. "I'm a much better alternative than going out there alone. It's dark, and there are camels."

She knew she was coming off crazy, but she giggled again. Being afraid of innocuous camels was the furthest thought from her mind.

"Lots of killer camels in this part of the country, I hear," she said. He stood back slightly as she mustered the energy to get out of bed. She lost track of how long she had been there, but it must have been a long time because her legs felt wobbly.

"You have no idea. They should really be outlawed, but they contribute to a lot of political campaigns, if you know what I'm saying. The camels have clout, no doubt about that."

"Most of what you say is nonsense, huh?" she said. She was finally standing, and she only wobbled a little.

"You catch on quick, Shelby Whatsits."

"It's Lance, Shelby Lance."

"Hey, I'm a lance corporal. Maybe we're related," Kelsey said.

"Could be. My dad's a general. Works at the pentagon."

His jaw dropped and his blinks became fast and furious as he sifted their conversation to see if he had said anything that could get him court martialed.

"Wow, you're shallow and gullible—the perfect combination," Shelby said. "The closest my father has ever come to the armed forces is catching candy the veterans throw at parades."

"You tricked me. And I was going to let you feel my biceps. No more. Your loss."

She would have laughed, but the pain in her midsection that had previously been a dull ache was now a sharp stab that increased with every step. By the time she reached the outhouse, she wanted to cry from the agony. What was wrong with her? What did they do to her?

"It's basically a hole in there," Kelsey said, sounding concerned once again. "Are you going to be able to support yourself?"

She would have to because she would die before she let him come into the bathroom with her. "Yes," she said.

"Good." He scanned the horizon. She didn't know what he was doing until he leaned in and spoke in a whisper. "Don't tell anyone what you're about to see here. I'm going to clue you in to my secret stash." He reached in his pocket and pulled out a moist wipe.

"You carry wet wipes?" she asked.

"Shh," he warned. "These are unsanctioned contraband, but I'm a delicate flower, and I need to take good care of me. What do I have if I don't have my beauty? Nothing. So use this, keep quiet about it, and I'll keep the supply coming for the duration of our stay here."

"Thank you," she whispered, all kidding aside. "It's very nice of you to share." He nodded and held the door for her while she hobbled inside. The smell was overpowering. There was a thumbnail moon, and no outside power to provide for flood lights or anything else, but Shelby was glad she couldn't see where she was. She had the feeling that the cleanliness of the main house didn't extend to this portion.

She thought maybe she had stopped bleeding, but when she hovered over the seat the now-familiar gushing sensation proved otherwise. How much more blood could she lose? And what would she do without any underpants to catch the flow? At least Kelsey had provided her with the one precious wipe. She could do as much repair work as she was able in the darkened shed. And the basin by the door of the yurt was for washing so she would at least be able to clean her hands when she was finished. Things weren't as bad as they could be, or so she tried to convince herself.

"Everything okay in there?" Kelsey asked.

"Fine," she lied. "I'm done." Grimacing, she tossed the wipe away and wished for a bath. She would need ten of them before she stopped feeling gritty and disgusting. She stepped out of the outhouse and swayed. Kelsey caught her, sweeping her up before she could topple forward. "Sorry," she murmured. She felt faint again and miserable. Being held by him wasn't anything like being held by Ashton. She wanted to tell him to set her down but realistically she knew she would probably keel over again. The helplessness made her frustrated and the frustration made her want to cry.

"It's no big deal. This happens to me a lot. I'm fairly swoonworthy. Women are always doing a header near me. It's my thing—I make women faint. To be honest, I would be insulted if you didn't pass out in my presence. I've sort of come to expect it."

He was trying hard to make her feel better, and she was trying hard to let him, but it wasn't working. She didn't want to be carried back to the yurt like an invalid. She didn't want them to have to stay here because of her. She wanted to walk under her own steam, to forge ahead like she was one of them and could carry her own weight.

They reached the house. He deposited her on the bed and she tensed, frustrated all over again by her newly developed fear of men. "Get some sleep Shelby Whatsits," he said, backing away as one might ease away from an angry bear—hands out, tone soft, working hard to show he was non-aggressive.

Shelby almost reminded him her last name was Lance, and then she realized he didn't care; he didn't want to know her. He wanted her to remain a part of the job, and she understood. But at the same time she longed for Ashton. Ashton was one of those people who always seemed to say the worst possible thing in a delicate situation, and yet everything he had said to her had been exactly what she needed to hear. Or maybe he wouldn't say anything at all. Maybe he would simply hold her and she would find a few minutes of security and peace in this never-ending nightmare.

Come back, Ashton, she silently pled. Then she did what Kelsey suggested and fell back asleep.

* * *

IF ASHTON COULD HAVE HEARD Shelby's unspoken plea, he would have felt heartened. As it was, he felt frustrated. The task of finding a usable radio wasn't as simple as it should have been. In a perfect world, he and Lolly would have walked into the nearest city, noticed an antennae sticking from a building, and known that was the place. In the real world everyone in Turkmenistan had discovered satellite. There were high rise buildings with dozens and dozens of satellites hanging from the windows and antennae littering the rooftops. It was disconcerting somehow to realize how remote they were, and yet behind those doors half the country was probably on Facebook. And if Truck and Lolly made the wrong move or trusted the wrong person then their picture would be all over Facebook, leaving the US Marine Corps to explain why two marines in battle dress uniforms suddenly strolled into Turkmenistan while a warlord in the making had his head blown off not too far away.

Coincidence wouldn't work as an excuse, not in a world that received their information almost before it happened. "I miss the old days," Truck whispered. Marines in World War II never had to worry about their picture being taken by some German national and spread all over the world at the speed of light.

"Cheer up, Grandpa, it's almost over," Lolly whispered. He pointed to a building, the last one on their list. They had split up to do recon—basically breaking into every building with an antennae to search for a radio. There was one left, and they would do it together.

"Why is it always in the last place we look?" Truck asked.

"Murphy's law of military recon," Lolly said. "What's the point of being a marine if everything is easy?"

"You are way too optimistic for someone who hasn't slept in two days," Truck informed him.

Lolly grinned. "You're looking a little cheerful yourself, lover boy."

"Let's go before you break into song like a cartoon character. Any other team would have killed you by now. You're too comfortable talking about feelings. Man up, Private, and become more dysfunctional."

"Aye, sir," Lolly said, feigning gravity as he appeared to be mulling Truck's words. "Though with you and Whit down for the count, I only have Jaw's dysfunction to emulate."

"That's okay—Kelsey has enough dysfunction for the whole world."

"True story," Lolly agreed. They went silent as they slipped into the building. It wasn't locked—nothing here was locked—so the real trick was avoiding detection, which was easier said than done in a country that thrived on social interaction. There were people everywhere, and they were friendly and chatty. Thankfully they were usually so involved in conversation they didn't notice the marines slinking behind them. The cover of night helped, as did the fact that people were winding down for the evening and readying for bed. With any luck when they found the radio its owner would be fast asleep.

Luck, however, was not on their side. After a half hour of sifting the building, they located the radio in an interior apartment. This door was locked, which wasn't a problem. But the radio's owner was sitting in front of it, talking. He went speechless as the two marines slipped into his house and hovered over him. They hadn't drawn their weapons, but they didn't need to. One wrong move on his part and he would be dead before he hit the floor.

"We need to use your radio," Truck said, trying Arabic first to see if the man understood him. The national language was Turkmen, but most people this close to the border also spoke Arabic. The man continued to stare in stunned silence, so Truck repeated the phrase in Russian and finally Turkmen. That was when he realized the man was in shock. The wet spot in his pants bore further testament to that fact, so Lolly stepped forward and immobilized him, applying his fingers to the pressure point in his neck until he became unconscious.

"Have a nice nap," Lolly whispered as he moved the man aside. Truck stepped forward and entered the transmission key. They had each memorized it in case they were separated, but Truck's grasp of all things mechanical made him better suited to handle the radio while Lolly's grasp of all things lethal made him a better guard.

Now wasn't the time to find out what had gone wrong with the other chopper, though Truck was curious. What he said to Shelby about going with the flow and changing plans at a moment's notice was true, but it wasn't often that their pickup was aborted. In fact it had only happened one other time, right before a skirmish had erupted that eventually turned into a civil war. The area where they had been hadn't seemed like a hotbed of unrest. In fact it had seemed deserted until the goons and Shelby showed up.

That left the option of political unrest in the United States. Wars were fought in Washington every day with policy makers handing down edicts, regardless of how it affected men on the ground. After so many years of being caught in the crosshairs, Truck was cynical. He didn't do what he did for the politicians, that was for certain. Not for the first time he wished they could spend a day in his world to understand how their bureaucracy affected real people. It was likely their mission had come to the attention of someone who didn't agree with it and their pickup was scrubbed while the higher ups slugged it out. Meanwhile the job was done and five people were stuck, waiting to go home. On a normal day, Truck would have tamped down his frustration, bottling it up with all the other things he couldn't control in life. But this time Shelby was affected, and he was angry.

But now wasn't the time for anger—it was the time for facts. He gave the coordinates of the place Shelby and the rest of the team were located, but his request was refused. Instead he was given return coordinates in the opposite direction. He rebutted, informing the base there was an injury and they needed a pickup where the person was located, but he was denied again. At last he threw down the controls in disgust. They would have to hike back to the hut at the edge of the desert and somehow get Shelby to the pickup location.

"Why can't anything ever go the way it's supposed to?" he asked. He tossed a five dollar bill on the unconscious man still lying on the floor.

Lolly watched. "You're going soft on me."

"Not his fault the higher ups are yanking our chains." Plus he felt they owed the guy something for knocking him out and causing him to soil his pants. He might continue to be terrified of American soldiers, but at least he wouldn't be able to say they cheated him by using his equipment for free. That was the impression he tried to use when dealing with civilians: Marines were the toughest, the bravest, and the best, but fair and compassionate, too. It was at times a heavy burden to feel like you might be someone's only impression of an entire country.

"Do you have any objection to booking it?" he asked Lolly as soon as they were free of the building. The hut was eleven miles away. With breaks, they could make it in less than two hours if they ran.

Lolly shrugged and shook his head, probably because he was too exhausted for anything else, and they took off.

Ashton was always amused by the people who took running so seriously, who pursued it as a hobby and poured their energy into learning how to do it better. For him running was a way of life, an integral part of the job. While others trained for months to run a half marathon, hoofing it eleven miles over rocky terrain was another day in paradise. Not to say he wasn't winded and lacking energy, because he was. He was minus a few thousand calories on this mission, to say nothing of the endless hours of sleep he needed to catch up on. But that was another part of the job—pushing himself to his physical limits and then a little bit more. Learning to be a marine meant learning to turn off the mental chatter that told you that you couldn't do something. Instead you did it. Go for days without food or sleep and still make split-second life-or-death decisions like a pro? No problem. Walk for hours through a steaming desert wasteland only to turn around and sprint eleven miles? Bring it. Pick up an injured civilian and somehow try to keep your heart intact? That one was a little trickier.

He had shoved thoughts of Shelby away to focus on his task, but the job was done and he had nothing to do for the next two hours but move his legs up and down. His mind had to dwell somewhere; might as well be on her. She had come out of nowhere and taken him by surprise, as had his response to her. He had gone from loathing to grudging acceptance to reluctant friendship to...what? He might as well admit that he had somehow fallen in love with her, which was crazy considering she was about as low as a person could be right now. What was worse was that he couldn't seem to muster any panic over the situation. Maybe being a marine had started to leak into his personal life, too, because he saw the challenge of loving Shelby and thought *bring it*.

The thought of seeing her again, holding her, and making sure she was okay put more speed into his jog. He glanced back to see if Lolly was keeping up.

"I'm really beginning to hate people who are in love," Lolly yelled. Then he found his own burst of energy and caught up with Truck.

CHAPTER 12

When Shelby woke, Ashton was beside her. She had no idea how long he had been there or how he had sneaked in without disturbing her, especially because he was still wearing his boots and multi-faceted belt. He smelled worse than before, as if he had bathed in sweat, but she didn't care. He was back, he had returned unharmed. It was strange how happy she was to see him. She had the irrational desire to wake him up to talk to him, but she refrained—especially because the other one, Lolly, was asleep in the corner.

In the kitchen someone was stirring. By the sounds of pots and utensils, Shelby thought maybe Dursun was preparing breakfast. The longer she lay there staring at the ceiling, the more she realized she had to use the bathroom again. As quietly as she could, she eased away from Truck's side and rolled off the mattress. Tiptoeing on legs that weren't quite steady, she slipped out of the room.

Dursun nodded and smiled at her, returning to her work of preparing breakfast. Shelby would have muttered a good morning because it was one of the handful of Arabic phrases she knew, but she didn't want to risk waking the other inhabitants of the house.

Nick and Kelsey were outside, their heads close together as if they were having a serious discussion. Their eyes flew to her when the door opened, revealing the fact that they were still wary despite Dursun's hospitality. When they realized it was her, Nick smiled and Kelsey left their huddle to come talk to her.

"Need any help getting there?" he nodded toward the ramshackle outhouse.

Shelby grimaced and shook her head. She would have to see the thing in the light of day now; she definitely wasn't ready for that.

"Call if you need help," Kelsey said. He stuck out his hand, waiting for her to shake it. She took and he passed her the wet wipe like a prospective diner passing the maître d' a tip. She smiled and he winked and the interaction made things feel almost normal, if normal was walking through the sand to reach a barely-there building whose stench hit her a dozen feet before she arrived.

She closed her eyes, not wanting to look at what would undoubtedly turn her stomach. Then she opened the door and things got worse because she heard the sound of something splashing from down below. *Rats.* Or maybe snakes. Whatever it was, it almost caused her to turn around and go back out again, but there was nowhere else to go. It was either have a small measure of privacy in the outhouse or try and duck out of sight of Dursun and the two soldiers roaming the perimeter. At this point a small shred of privacy and pride were all she had left, so she closed her eyes, blocked out the sounds and smells and did what she needed to do as fast as humanly possible.

There was only a small amount of blood today, and she allowed herself to rejoice over that fact. The end was almost near; Ashton and Lolly had returned and that meant they had arranged a helicopter. As she stood and righted her robes she thought how much she had previously feared and dreaded flying, and she suppressed the odd desire to chuckle. Right now being afraid to fly seemed like the stupidest thing on the planet. She had lived through hell—there was no room left to fear being suspended above the ground.

"Shelby, honey, you okay in there?"

It was Ashton. Shelby pushed back her semi-hysterical urge to laugh and used the clean portion of the wipe she had saved to wash her hands and face, feeling suddenly aflutter with nerves. "I'm fine. Did I wake you? I'm sorry."

"No, I woke up and noticed you were gone. I was, um, worried." He sounded as nervous as she felt. She wished she was making a better entrance than stepping from a stinky latrine, but there was no help for it. She stepped out, trying to pretend she was stepping from her room at home wearing makeup, clothes that fit, and good-smelling perfume. The effect was ruined when she stumbled a little and almost fell. He rushed forward and put out a hand to catch her, but stopped short when he realized she had righted herself.

"Hey," she said.

"Hey," he replied. They stood a foot apart, staring at each other, feeling inexplicably nervous, as if they were meeting up again after a year's absence instead of a few hours.

"How did the job go?"

"Good. We'll fill you in on the plan once Jaws and Whit finalize it. How was it here? Kelsey talk you to death?"

"No, it was fine. I slept." She clasped her hands behind her back and took another step forward, more to get away from the commode than to be near him. He didn't back up, and she took that as a good sign. "Dursun is cooking breakfast," she added, unnecessarily because he had no doubt passed Dursun on his way out here.

"I'm hungry," he said.

Their budding intimacy had been interrupted by his departure, and neither of them knew how to get it back. Maybe it was gone forever. Shelby bit her lip, "Ashton," she said.

"Shelby," he started at the same time. They realized they were speaking over top of each other and paused, smiling. "Ladies first," he prompted.

"I was going to say you've been so nice, and taken such good care of me. I think maybe I'm on the mend. I don't want you to feel obligated to see to my needs anymore. I've established a bit of a rapport with Nick and Kelsey; it doesn't bother me to be near them as much." Would he read between the lines of what she was trying to say? It was unfair to make him try and decipher her hidden meaning, but she couldn't come out and tell him she didn't want him as a caretaker; she wanted more.

"That's good. They're good guys, and they'll take good care of you. Lolly, too." She thought that was the end of his speech, and her heart sank until he took a couple of steps toward her, closing the gap between them as he reached out and drew her into his arms. "But I'm not going anywhere, Shelby. Don't let the situation confuse my feelings for you. When this is over, we're going to sort things out between us." He leaned down, but he didn't kiss her. He simply rested his forehead on hers and looked into her eyes, searching for a response through the windows of her soul.

"Okay," she said, an understatement if there ever was one, but she was confused. The timing couldn't have been worse; she wasn't exactly in the best place for a relationship right now. In fact, there had never been a worse time to meet someone. Maybe she was losing it because she started to laugh again. Not an amused sound, but a nervous chuckle—a sound she had never made before.

"What?" Truck asked, smiling in confusion.

"Seriously, has the timing ever been worse for anyone in the world than it is right now?" What did it say about her life that she met the perfect guy only after being kidnapped and dragged into the desert?

"No argument here: the timing stinks. But I think you and I could be really great." His thumb brushed the side of her cheek. Even covered in remnants of camo paint he was nice looking, but that wasn't what attracted her to him. His heart was huge, despite how much time he spent pretending to be closed off from the rest of the world.

"Yo, you guys ready for breakfast?" Kelsey poked his head around the side of the yurt, undaunted by finding them in a tight embrace, but Shelby was thankful for the interruption. She was sick, body, mind, and soul—not the best time to be making major life decisions.

Ashton gave him a heads-up nod and he disappeared.

"Could we maybe talk more about this later?" Shelby asked.

"Take all the time you need, Shelby. I realize this is too much to lay at your feet right now and, like I said, I'm not going anywhere."

Except he was. In a few short hours they would board a helicopter and he would deliver her to the hospital in Germany. Who knew when they would see each other again? Even if they lived in the same state, which they didn't, he was gone for long periods of time. He couldn't allow that to matter, though. It had taken him almost a decade to start living and feeling again; he wasn't going to lose her to a little thing like geography or a big thing like the trauma she had suffered. One way or another, things would work out. They had to.

Getting back to the yurt should have been a relief. Since he was the only one who could fluently converse with Dursun, it would be up to him to carry on polite conversation over breakfast. It should have been a chance to compartmentalize thoughts about Shelby and concentrate on idle chatter. But Dursun wanted to talk about Shelby, about their life together in the states, and their future plans. If the cover story he had told her was true, then it would have been a happy topic for a newlywed. As it was, plotting his fake life with his pretend bride was painful.

"She's never seen my house," he said, glad that at least one part of the story was truthful. "We live together." He pointed to his teammates.

Dursun clucked her tongue. "No new bride wants to live with a bunch of men. Believe me, I had to live with my husband's six brothers when I was a new bride."

"He's moving anyway," he said, referring to Nick. He swirled his yogurt absently while he talked. Dursun only had enough utensils for Shelby, but that was okay; that's why God made fingers.

"There's still much pain in your wife's eyes," Dursun observed. "Are you sure taking her from her family is wise?"

"Her family hurts her. They don't mean to, but she's different than they are. I think…I think I can do a better job taking care of her." He wasn't sure he was pretending anymore. Being near Shelby's family *was* painful for her, and he *could* take care of her.

"Every young person thinks their family is horrible until they move away. Then they realize how much they love and need their family. My own daughter was happy to move to the city, and now she sends me letters, 'Mama, Mama, I miss you. Come visit me.' Bah," she waved her hand. "Children."

Ashton smiled as he watched her bustle around the small space. She was a matronly woman, if somewhat domineering. It was easy to imagine her as someone's mother. "I think she'll be happy with me."

"I suppose it doesn't matter now; it is your responsibility to take care of her."

"It's not that it's my responsibility; it's that I love her," Ashton said.

"You are a young man and do not yet realize that love isn't what you think. When I was a young girl and full of dreams, I didn't think I would be living with a camel trader on the edge of the desert." She gestured around the yurt. "But life hands you choices, and you cope with them as they come. And that is where you find love—in the day to day living."

"Dursun, you're a poet," Ashton teased.

"Bah," she said, waving her hand at him again, but as she turned back to the fire pit, she was smiling. "My husband will never believe me when I tell him what took place while he was in the city visiting his brothers. He thinks I am a doddering old woman good for nothing but milking the camels. Wait until I tell him that four American soldiers slept here!" He watched the blush of excitement steal into her cheeks and wondered how old she was. She looked seventy, but that might have been from too much sun and hard work. She was probably closer to her fifties.

There were times, like now, when he was confronted with women the same age as his mother would have been, and the sight was painful to him. He couldn't help but compare and wonder what his mother would have been like if she had lived. Would she have straightened her life out? She had been motherly in her way, never throwing him under the bus like Nick's mother had done. His earliest understanding of his mother was that she loved him, but she was sick. Maybe with time and treatment she might have gotten better. She could have been like Dursun, a grandmotherly woman who rarely left her house. There was a good chance she would have been an excellent grand-mother since being a grandparent required all of the love with none of the responsibility. His mother hadn't been short on love, just good care and common sense.

Breakfast ended. They boiled water and refilled their bottles, adding iodine as a secondary precaution. Dursun packed bread and dates for their lunch while Shelby went into the bedroom to put on her shoes. Dursun watched her go, clucking her tongue in disapproval.

"She shouldn't be walking on those feet," she explained. "I bathed and swaddled them while she was sleeping, but they haven't healed yet."

Frowning, Truck followed Shelby into the room. She was sitting at the side of the mattress, unwinding the bindings from her feet. Truck hadn't noticed them before. "Let me see your feet," he commanded.

She jumped and shifted guiltily away. "They're fine," she said.

Ignoring her he knelt and finished unwrapping the bandages. "Oh, Shelby," he said when they were revealed. They were swollen and lacerated to bloody pulps. They had blistered, the blisters had erupted, and new blisters had formed on top of those. He picked up her shoes and studied them. They were unserviceable sandals, more suited for walking around the house than trouncing through the desert. Sand was a harsh exfoliant. It had done a number on Shelby, eviscerating her skin. "Honey, you can't walk on these. We'll carry you."

"No." It was the first time she had come close to snapping at him. She ripped the sandal out of his hand and began to put it on, but he stopped her.

"Shelby, you can't walk."

"I can, and I will."

"Shelby," he pressed.

She took a breath, held it, and let it out slowly as if trying to still her overwrought emotions. "I have one ounce of pride left, Ashton, and it's all that's keeping me together. This desire to walk under my own steam is the last stop between me and a total breakdown. I have to walk. I'll be okay."

"It's far," he said. He felt like he was the one about to have a breakdown. It wasn't enough that she was bleeding inside, but her feet had to be a pulpy mess, too.

"It's okay," Shelby said. They were close together with her siting and him kneeling. She put her arms around his head and drew him against her, and he let her. It was an odd thing to be comforted by someone who was so in need of comfort herself. He was strong and capable of taking care of her, but the reverse was true, too. She might be in the worst shape of her life, but she still had love and tenderness to bestow. It wasn't all about her and her needs as he had feared it would be if he ever let down his guard enough to accept someone into his life.

He slipped his arms around her and clung. He wasn't certain then which of them was giving comfort and which was receiving. Maybe it was mutual. All he knew was that the hug was restorative, and when they broke apart they each felt a little more able to face what was to come. Though if they knew what was to come, they might not have been so quick to smile and help each other off the floor; they might never have left Dursun's at all.

CHAPTER 13

*D*ursun kissed her goodbye.

It was another of those almost breaking points for Shelby, another moment when she threw her arms around the older woman and clung, barely able to hold back the barrage of tears that was getting harder and harder to control. She felt like the little boy with his finger in the dam, barely containing a consuming flood of grief.

Dursun took Shelby's face in her hands and said something that had the tone of a blessing. Shelby waited to ask Ashton to translate until they were safely away from the house.

"She said you are filled with youth, beauty, and the promise of love. But someday those things will be gone and only what is inside you will matter, so concentrate on enriching your life with joy and laughter and eventually they will take the place of sadness."

She sniffled, allowing one solitary tear to escape for the sweet woman and her beautiful words. Then she painfully swallowed the rest back down—a feat that was getting harder to accomplish each time she did it. But now wasn't the time. Now they had to trudge a few more hours to the pickup site, and she was already slowing the team's progress. Her feet were beyond hurting. Shelby was thankful for the numbness. It felt like walking on dead stumps. If only whatever was wrong inside of her was as numb, then she could walk much faster. As it was, her insides ached, a sharp, stabbing pain that caught her breath and made her eyes water. She forced herself not to think about the pain, not to think about anything.

Ashton didn't hold her hand, and she was glad. Either he sensed her need to draw into herself for self-preservation or he simply didn't want to hold onto her, she didn't know. And she didn't care. It was all she could do to put one foot in front of the other. Survival had become her mantra. *Rightfootleftfootrightfootleftfoot,* was all she would allow herself to think at present. There would be time to deal with everything else later, always later.

* * *

HE WAS WORRIED ABOUT HER. She was stumbling forward like a zombie. Ashton had observed that same look on victims of disaster. They came away from destroyed homes after losing everything, stumbling through the rubble like walking wounded—eyes glazed, brain off, feelings dead. They were in more danger than the actual wounded because they tended not to notice their surroundings. They stepped on nails, walked into burning buildings, tripped over barbed wire. It was as if they were sleepwalking, and now Shelby had that same look, like someone who had died inside, and it scared him. Worse, he didn't know how to help her. The feeling of helplessness harkened him back to his youth with his mother. What if he didn't get Shelby to help in time? What if she was permanently damaged by everything that had happened to her? What if she died?

He shook his head like a wet dog trying to shake off water. No. Shelby wouldn't die. He would get her to safety, get her the help she needed, and after that...well, after that was anyone's guess. But he wasn't giving up on her, wasn't letting her go. Somehow, some way, they would make it through and find a way to be together.

* * *

NICK WAS WORRIED. An optimist by nature, worry didn't feel natural. Sometimes it couldn't be helped, like now when Kelsey was quiet—that was always a bad sign. And the usually unruffled Truck barely had his head in the game. Then there was Shelby whose misery was weighing them all down because they were helpless to fix her. Only Lolly seemed to be his usual ninja self, scanning the horizon as he walked ten paces ahead, his rifle held aloft—the consummate point man.

The new landing zone was one more kink in a mission gone awry. Who knew finding and eliminating his target would be the easiest part of the assignment? Getting out was proving to be improbable, if not impossible. Nick was as frustrated as Truck over the change, but unlike Truck he couldn't let his anger show. He had to be the leader, to suck up his feelings, and roll with the punches as if hiking for miles to reach the chopper had been his plan all along. Inside, though, he was seething. Part of his anger was directed at himself. If he hadn't waited to go to Officer Candidate School, if he had done it years ago when he finished his degree, then maybe he would have been able to pull rank and demand a pickup closer to Dursun's hut.

As it was he had allowed fear to hold him back, which meant he was still a lowly corporal, taking orders from some higher up who had no idea the way his arbitrary commands were affecting the men on the ground. Nick promised himself that when he became an officer, he would be different. He wouldn't forget what it meant to be a grunt doing the hands-on work. And he wouldn't kowtow to the higher ups in Washington, either. Not if it meant throwing good soldiers under the bus in the process. Who cared about promotions when the lives of men and women were on the line?

Then again, didn't everyone have these thoughts before they became an officer? No one went to Officer Candidate School because he wanted to be a suck-up yes-man. Everyone probably believed he would be different. He felt a moment of panic until he remembered his secret weapon: Ashleigh. Ashleigh would never let him get away with being a tool. She would say it in a nicer way, but she would let him know if he was becoming a puppet or forgetting the little guy.

He smiled, thinking of his plain-spoken, feisty, yet soft-hearted fiancée. She had already changed him—for the better, he hoped. There was a time when he would have insisted they carry Shelby to hurry things along. Not because they were in danger of missing their flight, but because he was impatient for the mission to be over. But since Ashleigh he thought more about the human element involved in any assignment. It was important to Shelby to walk, to maintain that last bit of dignity. And if it was important to Shelby, then it was important to Truck who had somehow fallen for her completely. So they would plod slowly instead of sprint because what did it matter when they arrived as long as they arrived in one piece?

KELSEY WAS likewise thinking of Ashleigh, or rather Ashleigh's pot roast. The woman could cook, no disputing that. Melly could cook, but not in the way he liked. Her cooking was more likely to burn the buds off his tongue and, despite being adventurous in most areas of his life, he was not an adventurous eater. Give him regular old beef and potatoes seven days a week and twice on Sunday. He wasn't even much of a pizza fan. In fact he was a picky eater, something that drove Melly crazy. Only ravenous hunger had forced him to swallow the goat and yogurt at Dursun's house, that and good manners. He generally ate whatever was put before him like a good soldier, but that didn't mean he liked it. So while Truck was focused on Shelby and Nick was thinking about Ashleigh, Kelsey was daydreaming about meat with all the trimmings. Somehow he would have to find a way to be invited to Nick's coming home dinner because Ashleigh always made one, and it was always epic. Maybe if he innocently showed up uninvited she would take pity on him; it wasn't the most dignified way of getting what he wanted, but he had used it before, and he would probably use it again. What did the process matter if the end result was beef in his belly?

* * *

SHELBY HAD LOST all sense of time and place. It seemed they had been walking for hours, but maybe it was only a few minutes. Had Ashton given her food and water to drink, or had she imagined that part? She didn't know. Everything was numb, even her lips no longer burned and chafed. She was so numb she felt like she could probably keep doing this forever. She felt nothing, less than nothing, and in an odd way it was almost a relief. All she had to do was put one foot in front of the other endlessly and all her feelings were held at bay. No emotional or physical trauma was able to intrude as long as she kept walking, but Ashton's voice interrupted her mental haze, pulling her back to the surface again.

"We're almost there, Shelby. Over that summit, and we're there. We're lining up with the time, too. We won't have to stand and wait for a long time. A few more feet, and we're golden."

Shelby nodded, only half noting what he said. She did notice the tension in his voice. Was it for her or because of the obscuring rocks that now stood between them and the landing zone? For the last few hours, the landscape had been flat, unmarred by structures or civilization of any kind. It was almost like being back in the desert except the ground was more compact and the sun less punishing. A vague part of her brain, the one that used to be a girl scout, thought maybe they were heading east. Since she didn't know where they were, though, it didn't really matter where they were heading. All that mattered was getting home, and now their view was obscured by a large rock formation that looked like it had either once been the beginning or the ending of a building. Was it a scrapped design or the remains of what had once stood? She couldn't tell. Maybe there weren't any rocks at all. Maybe she was hallucinating.

The sudden tension wasn't her imagination, though. She could feel it prickling her skin. Her heartbeat kicked up painfully in response and she found herself scanning the horizon as the other men were doing, although she had no idea what she was looking for.

They edged closer to her at the exact moment that Lolly stopped, his hand held aloft in the sign Truck had taught her meant "halt." For one split second everyone froze, and then the world erupted into chaos.

Lolly turned around. "Go back," he yelled, and then he dropped to the ground in a stunning rain of gunfire. Shelby jumped, startled by the loud sound. A second later she was on the ground, Ashton on top of her, as a group of men began streaming from behind the rocks. There was too much motion for her to understand what was happening. All she knew was that men, bullets, and gunfire were everywhere. There were shouts. Some part of her mind recognized the voices of her captors, and she knew they had been ambushed by the men who had taken her. But her brain couldn't seem to grasp the threads of what was going on. Maybe that was a mercy, though, because some of the cries turned to anguish, and she knew men were being killed.

"The chopper is here," Ashton said in her ear, his voice urgent. "I have to go take care of this, but I'm going to cover you. When I get up, I want you to go. Don't stop until you reach it. Run, Shelby, okay, run."

She nodded, but she wasn't sure the words made sense. *Run.* She focused on that one. She could run. He pointed toward the direction she should go, and then his reassuring weight was off her and she was exposed. For the tiniest second she remained, confused, but then her adrenaline kicked in and told her what to do. *Run.* She stood and began sprinting toward where she knew the chopper would be. She couldn't see it yet, but she trusted it was there.

But she hadn't taken more than twenty steps when she stopped again because Lolly was in her path, and there was no way she could pass by him without stopping to help. There was a lot of blood beneath him, but he was conscious. He frowned at her.

"Don't stop," he commanded, his breath coming in short, sharp gasps. "Go. Run."

She didn't, though. She couldn't leave him there, exposed for anyone who had a mind to come back and finish him off. So she circled her arms around his torso and began laboriously dragging him toward the helicopter. She could hear it now, the blades cutting the air with a heavy *thwack, thwack, thwack.* The sound was different than news or medical helicopters she had seen. This was a military heli-copter, and it was huge.

They were making progress when the man caught up to him. He was one of her captors, one who had brutalized her as much as any of the others, and when he reached them there was a gleeful sort of grin on his face. Shelby didn't stop, but it didn't matter. They were making snail's progress. What good was an injured marine and a defenseless woman against so much evil?

The man raised his gun, but both of them had underestimated Lolly who did the same thing. Lolly squeezed the trigger, and the man went down. But so did Shelby and Lolly. She hadn't known he was going to shoot and hadn't braced herself for the gun's recoil. It slammed through Lolly and into her, and now he was lying on top of her, his blood soaking her robe. She began inching from beneath him when he was suddenly lifted off. She screamed until she realized the man now carrying Lolly was American. He said something, but she couldn't hear him. Logic told her he was from the helicopter. When he beckoned her in that direction, she followed.

He deposited Lolly on the chopper, helped her inside, and faced the direction of the skirmish. It was clear he intended to go and help, but he had barely taken a few steps when the remaining three team members ascended the summit, Truck limping between Nick and Kelsey as they held him aloft. Shelby suppressed a gasp, knowing hysteria wouldn't help the situation. At least Ashton was upright, which was more than she could say for Lolly. She was holding his hand, but his grasp was weak, his breathing strained.

They reached the aircraft and lifted Ashton inside. He scooted to Shelby and wordlessly surveyed her as she did the same to him. "I'm okay," she told him, noting as she did so that there was blood pouring from his knee. "You were shot," she said, making it a statement instead of a question.

He gave a curt nod, one that told her he was in a whole lot of pain.

"Let's go," Nick told the pilot. He sounded grim and angry. "You're going to need to order a cleanup back there. About a dozen insurgents on the ground."

"Any of them still alive?" the pilot asked as he picked up his radio.

"No," Nick said, and he didn't sound sorry.

They took off and attention shifted to Lolly. The bottom of the helicopter was slick with his blood. Or maybe it was Ashton's blood—he was losing a fair amount through the wound in his leg. Shelby tore off a piece of her robe and went to work trying to staunch the bleeding while Ashton stared at Lolly, worry written all over his features.

Nick and Kelsey were on each side of the smaller marine. Nick carefully removed his vest, his hands trembling as he peeled it away to survey the damage. "It's bad," Lolly gasped.

"It's not so bad," Nick said, giving him a reassuring smile that didn't quite reach his eyes.

"You're going to be fine, kid," Kelsey added.

Lolly turned his head, searching for Ashton. "Truck?"

Ashton dragged himself closer and surveyed the damage. "It's bad," he said, swallowing hard when his voice broke. Shelby skittered behind him, still attempting to stop his forgotten leg from bleeding. She didn't want to look at Lolly, didn't want to know how badly he was hurt, but she couldn't help it. He was right beside her now, and even if she hadn't seen the damage to his chest, she would have heard the liquid in his lungs as he strained to breathe.

"You're going to be fine," Kelsey reiterated. Ashton shouldered him aside and reached in Lolly's pocket. Pulling out his rosary, he stuffed it in the younger marine's hand, curling his fingers around it.

"Take care of Melly," Lolly commanded Kelsey.

"There's no need..." Kelsey began, but Lolly interrupted.

"Swear it, swear you'll take care of Melly."

"I'll take care of Melly, you know I will," Kelsey said. "But..."

"Swear," Lolly prodded.

"I swear I'll take care of Melly, but there's no need for this. You're going to be fine," Kelsey said. He was colorless, his pupils dilated to the size of pennies. Shelby searched him up and down for blood, but he wasn't wounded. At least not physically.

On Lolly's other side, Nick grasped his hand and it was clear he was working hard not to cry. He began gently rocking back and forth, breathing almost as hard as Lolly as he tried to rein in his emotions. To Shelby's surprise, Lolly looked at her. Clutching the cross on his rosary, he held it upright in her direction.

"Don't lose faith, Shelby," he commanded.

She shook her head. "I won't," she promised. Reaching out, she rested her hand on his leg. It was shaking.

Lolly's gaze rested on Ashton. "Last rites," he said.

"I swear. You know there are priests everywhere in Germany. I'll find one, I promise," Truck said. He reached out and rested his hand on Lolly, too, as if sealing the oath.

Speaking was becoming more difficult. Lolly surveyed the small group, lingering on each man. "Love…" he gasped. "My brothers." He closed his eyes then, and the sound was unbearable, like listening to someone drown. His chest heaved upward with the effort, his head tipped backward like some invisible force was tugging at him. There was no medical equipment on the helicopter, nothing that could help him but a surgeon and a tank of oxygen. The feeling of hopelessness was overwhelming. From the rosary and last rites request, Shelby guessed he was catholic. She wasn't sure what their traditions were or what hymns they sang, but she decided to sing anyway, a soft rendition of *Amazing Grace.* Maybe it was wishful thinking on her part, but his breathing seemed to grow easier, his features less strained until at last he ceased breathing altogether. Shelby was in the middle of the fourth verse then. The words slowly faded away as silence descended over the group, broken only by the rotation of the blades and the crackling of the radio.

Shock, raw and tinged with grief and anger settled over the small space like a blanket. Shelby was crying; the men were breathing heavily as if they had run for miles. The flight still had hours to go. Shelby's side was becoming wet with Ashton's blood. She turned her attention to him, glad to have something to occupy her hands and mind. She had nowhere else to go, but she felt like an intruder in the aircraft. She barely knew the man on the floor, didn't even know his real name, and yet she grieved for him. How much more must the three men be grieving for the one who had been like a brother?

Nick was the only one who was crying. He wasn't making any attempt to stifle it or cry silently. Instead he rested his head on Lolly's bloody, still chest and sobbed violently, clinging to the younger man as if his tears could somehow restore life.

Kelsey looked pale and dazed, as if he had taken a significant blow to the head. Shelby wondered if he would need medical attention when they arrived in Germany. Ashton looked like he was trying hard not to be sick, either from the pain in his leg or the pain in his heart Shelby didn't know. She did the best she could of staunching his blood, but he didn't seem to notice. Instead he stared silently at Lolly, rocking gently back and forth like a baby who tries to sooth himself when his mother is away.

All too soon she finished her ministrations and then there was nothing to do. The aircraft was cold, and she shivered, looking away from the body on the floor. Before her kidnapping, she had never watched anyone die. Now she had seen three people lose their lives in the most violent manner possible. While she was too numb to feel much now, she had a feeling she would be dealing with the aftermath of such violence for a long, long time.

Ashton rested his hand on her shoulder, and she jumped. Her teeth began to chatter, and he reached for her, drawing her into his lap as he leaned against the side of the helicopter, careful to keep his injured leg to the side. He held her for the rest of the flight, not saying a word, clinging to her as she clung to him. She couldn't seem to stop shaking no matter how warm he was or how tightly he held her.

By the time they touched down in Germany everyone was quiet and subdued. Nick had stopped crying. Kelsey remained staring dully. Ashton had stopped rocking back and forth, and Shelby's teeth stopped chattering.

The aircraft set down lightly. The co-pilot came around to open the door and stood back as a medical team came with a stretcher. They stood in the opening of the helicopter, trying to determine who needed the most help. They all must have looked in rough shape, because it took them a long time to decide. At last they motioned for Shelby, but she shook her head.

"Take Lolly first," she demanded. "He requested last rites." And somehow she felt like he should go first so they could make sure he received the proper care and respect due him. She didn't know why, but waiting felt like the right thing.

The men in scrubs reached for him, and that's when Kelsey snapped back to life and lost it. "Don't touch him," he yelled, propelling himself at one of the men so he was knocked back against the wall of the chopper. Ashton barely pulled Shelby out of the way before she got smashed in the press of bodies. He winced with a sharply indrawn breath, a sign that he had probably re-injured his already injured leg.

Reinforcements began pouring out of the hospital. Some of them had weapons, but they weren't necessary. Nick leapt over Lolly and tackled Kelsey, holding him down with no small amount of difficulty.

"He's gone. Don't do this," he said, his tone both soft and commanding.

Kelsey couldn't speak with Nick cutting off his air supply, but he nodded. Nick let him go and they sat back, watching as the men loaded Lolly on a stretcher and covered his face.

"Make sure he gets a priest," Ashton said.

Nick scooted out of the chopper, keeping pace with the stretcher while Kelsey watched them go, the dazed look returning to his face.

Another stretcher came. Shelby started to insist that Ashton go next, but one look at his face told her that wouldn't be possible.

"Go," he commanded. Two men in scrubs reached in and took her arms to help her out as she glanced back at Ashton. "I'll find you as soon as I can," he promised.

She faced forward, allowing the men to help her out. One reached out to lift her onto the stretcher, and she shied away from him. "I'll climb up," she said. Some of her numbness began to give way to fear again. She didn't know these men, didn't have any idea where they were taking her. What if they didn't take her where they were supposed to? She was vulnerable and exposed. She closed her eyes and breathed deeply as they rolled. If she had looked out the window as they landed, she would have been relieved by the sight of the pristine white hospital, the largest American hospital outside the US. But she hadn't looked, and she wasn't reassured, not until a woman's voice spoke gently near her ear.

She opened her eyes to see a nurse standing beside her waiting to ask her questions, and she breathed a sigh of relief. "Don't leave me alone with them, please," she blurted.

"We'll make sure a woman is with you at all times whenever it's necessary for you to see a man, okay?" the woman said.

"Thank you."

Another stretcher rolled by and she knew before she saw him it was Ashton. There were too many people milling around to do more than look at each other, but he gave her a little wave. She smiled quaveringly in return.

"I'll find you," he mouthed.

She stared at him, numbness flowing through her.

Kelsey plodded slowly behind him. The double doors closed, but Shelby kept watching, long after they were out of sight.

CHAPTER 14

*I*t took three days for Ashton to make good on his promise to find Shelby. In that time he had surgery, and Shelby did, too. He knew because he overheard a couple of nurses whispering about her when they thought he was sleeping. The damage from the brutality was so extensive that it took a few hours of surgery to put her back together again. Ashton wished he could go back and kill her attackers all over again, not only for her, but for Lolly. He couldn't believe the little guy was gone. He kept expecting to see his head pop around the corner, a cheerful smile on his face. Instead he was in the morgue, his body in standby until the team could fly home tomorrow. They opted to stay together with Nick and Kelsey remaining behind while Ashton asked to go early in order to travel with the body. Lolly's body. Unbelievable.

The nurses wouldn't let him out of bed, so Nick retrieved a wheelchair for him and helped him into it. Moving hurt. A lot. But there was no way he was leaving without seeing Shelby, and the only way to do it was to go to her.

No one would tell them where she was. Subterfuge was generally Kelsey's specialty, but he was still out of commission, sitting in Truck's room and staring blankly at the floor day after day. So it was up to Nick to try and track down her room number, a task that took longer than it should have because Shelby was apparently spurring the protective instinct of all the women on the floor. Or maybe all the women in Germany. They were angry at what had been done to her, and since they couldn't retaliate directly, they took out their seething sense of injustice on all the men around them.

But the men were angry, too. Not only for Shelby, but for Nick and his team and the idiotic decision to move the landing zone farther inland. As Truck suspected, the decision had been a bureaucratic one. Someone in Washington decided to stick his thumb in the military pie and decree that a landing zone so close to the border might arouse hostility and suspicion; therefore it was better to land farther inside Turkmenistan, despite the fact that a four-man team plus an injured woman would have to walk for hours to reach it. Things that looked good on paper rarely worked out well in the field, but there was no use in wasting anger over the situation. It wasn't the first time such a mistake had happened, and it wouldn't be the last. There was a good chance whichever higher up made the decree would never even know he cost the life of a good man.

So Truck pushed aside his pain and rage and focused on getting to Shelby. Kelsey rallied at the end and created a diversion at one end of the hall, distracting the nurses and orderlies so Nick could roll Truck into Shelby's room.

She looked different than he was used to. The hijab was gone, and she had apparently showered because now her black hair was so shiny that it looked almost blue under the fluorescent lights. Her face was smudge free. She was startlingly beautiful, and yet her sadness and shock were palpable.

The shadows under her eyes were so deep they looked like bruises. Her dark skin somehow managed to look pale, her lips now healed but bloodless, as if the life had drained from her.

"Hey," Truck said, softly so as not to startle her.

She turned toward him, mustering a smile. "Hey."

"How're you doin'?" He rolled closer until his chair bumped the side of her bed.

"Okay. I'm on heavy-duty painkillers, so I'm not feeling much at all."

Maybe not physically, but the drugs were doing nothing to dull her emotional pain. Shelby was struggling, and his heart wrenched at the sight of her in so much pain. Like he had come to expect, though, she turned the focus on him.

"How are you, Ashton? They told me your knee is pretty bad." She bit her lip. "Your career..." she let the thought hang.

"It's fine." He squeezed her hand. "I'm definitely off active duty for a while, and I'm going to need some physical therapy, but I'll be back in no time."

"I'm sorry about Lolly," she said, her voice dropping to a whisper. "I can't help but feel like his death is my fault. If I hadn't been there, he might still be alive."

"If you hadn't been there, there still would have been that screwy changeup with the landing zone."

"Yes, but they were coming for me."

"We killed their leader. They were coming for retribution. There was no way they could have known you were with us. There's no blame in this for you. It was what it was, and Lolly knew the risks."

"I'm sorry all the same," she said.

"Me, too," he said. His voice broke and he wiped a tear. He hadn't grieved for Lolly yet. That would come later, when they were home and going through the process of laying him to rest.

"My family is coming. They should be here any time," she said. This time she was the one who broke. She let go his hand and covered her face as she finally, blessedly wept.

Truck used his arms to lever himself up, sliding in beside her so he could hold her. She crumpled, pressing her face to his chest as violent sobs shook her. She cried for a long, long time and then she lay back, exhausted. He reached over her to grab a tissue from beside then bed and then used it to wipe her face.

"I don't want to lose you," she blurted. "I don't want to say goodbye."

He froze, the tissue held in midair a second before he slowly began drying her face again. "Then don't. I've had a lot of time to think. Life is short, Shelby. It took me a decade to find you, to begin to feel again after my mother's death. I don't want to lose you, either. Come home with me. I can arrange for you to be on the flight with us tomorrow." He set the tissue aside and took her hands in his. "Come to North Carolina with me. I'll take care of you. We'll get better together." He didn't wait for her to answer. Instead he kissed her, and there was no mistaking this kiss for affection. It was passionate and romantic, and Shelby was shocked to find herself responding.

The kiss ended and her eyes remained closed, her hand pressed to his cheek. It was so tempting to say yes. She wanted to. She loved this man. She wanted to be with him almost as much as she didn't want to go home to Texas. Being in North Carolina would be easy in comparison, like running away to a place you knew you were welcome. She wouldn't have to face the looks of her family and friends as they speculated over how she was recovering. She wouldn't have to face the pity and speculation of acquaintances on the street of her small hometown. And she would be with Ashton. He would take care of her. He had already proved himself capable of meeting her needs, and he was good at it.

And there was the problem. Ashton had spent the first eighteen years of his life taking care of a wounded woman. Was it fair to make him do it again? No. Running away, while it may appear as the better action now, would only hurt her in the long run. Someday Ashton would resent her for making him take care of her. Maybe not now, but someday. And she wouldn't feel very proud of herself if she took the coward's way out.

"I can't," she said at last. She opened her eyes and saw pain in his. He didn't understand. He thought she was rejecting him.

"Shelby, I love you. You have to know that I love you," he said.

"I do," she said. She felt his love like a physical thing. The certainty of it went all the way to her bones, furthering her decision to protect him, to protect them. "And I love you, Ashton. But someone once told me I have a gift for perseverance. Following you to North Carolina, which would make me euphorically happy, would mean I was taking the easy way out. It would mean for the first time in my life that I was giving up. I have to go home. I have to heal, and you need to heal, too. Not just physically. There's a lot inside you that needs cleaned up."

He sighed. "And I thought you were going to be easy to manipulate to my way of thinking."

She smiled. "No such luck, I'm afraid. But I do want you in my life. Maybe we can keep in contact to make certain this thing that's between us is real."

"It is," he insisted.

"I think so, too. But we've got a lot of work to do before we see each other again." She bit her lip, waiting for him to take the next step. He didn't disappoint.

"I'm going to need a date for Ashleigh and Nick's wedding in a few months. Think you'll be available?"

"I could probably clear my schedule."

"If you come to North Carolina in a few months and things go well, will you stay?" he asked.

"That's definitely something to consider," Shelby said. She wanted to say yes, but she was on drugs. There was always the possibility that she wasn't thinking rationally. Best not to commit to a lifetime yet.

"I'm going to call you every day, or you're going to call me," Ashton said.

"Yes, Ashton, whatever you say, Ashton," Shelby said, the model of perfect submission he had earlier said he wanted.

"If I thought you really meant those words, I would call a preacher and marry you this very minute," Ashton said.

Shelby smiled, feeling a little bit lighter. She still faced the ordeal of seeing her family, and that would be hard. But she no longer felt like her world had fallen apart. In fact, maybe it had expanded. She had Ashton now, and that was something irrevocable she wouldn't have had without the horror of the last few days. However briefly she had known him, Lolly's bravery and faith had made an indelible impression. And then there was kindhearted Dursun who had worked to bring Shelby healing in her own humble way. When she stepped back and looked at her life that way, she could see how God had put people in her path to help her during her greatest time of need. Maybe He hadn't intervened to stop her from being attacked, but He would be with her in the aftermath; He would bring healing and peace. And she had promised Lolly—she could never lose hope, never lose faith.

"I'm going to be okay," she said with some confidence. "And you're going to be okay. We're going to be okay together."

"When you say it, I believe it," he said.

"When are you leaving?" she asked.

"A few hours. It's…it's going to be hard." Taking Lolly home this way wasn't what any of them wanted.

"I wish I could go and be with you and have it be the right decision," she said. "I want to, you know."

"I know." He also knew why she wasn't going, knew she was putting his wellbeing above her own by trying to save him from trying to fix her. She was right; going their separate ways for the time being was the right decision. But that didn't mean it was easy.

"Could you maybe stay with me for a while?" she asked.

"Only if your nurse guard doesn't come in and roust me out."

"They're trying to protect me from all the men of the world. I forgot to tell them there's an exception," Shelby said. She rested her head on his shoulder, her hand pressed to his chest. "I can feel your heartbeat," she commented. "I couldn't before, when you were wearing your vest."

"I can touch your hair. You don't wear a hijab at home, do you?" He had never asked her if she was actually Muslim.

"I would be the only Lutheran in my hometown to do so," she said. They had been through so much in such a short time. In some ways they knew each other better than anyone else, and in others they didn't know each other at all. "Ashton."

"Mmm."

He sounded sleepy. She felt sleepy, too. The drugs made her drowsy, but she hadn't been sleeping well. Now that he was nearby and she felt safe, she knew she was moments away from conking out. "When we see each other again, can we keep it as boring as possible? I've had enough excitement for a lifetime."

"Is it boring enough for you if we stay up all night talking?" he asked.

"Sounds perfect."

His hand began gently smoothing over her hair, twining in the long strands.

"Ashton," she murmured.

"Hmm," he replied.

"Maybe we could skip the talking next time and do this instead," she suggested.

"Yes, Shelby, whatever you say, Shelby," he whispered. His eyes were closed. A few minutes later he was asleep. She watched him for a little while, then she closed her eyes and followed suit.

EPILOGUE

Kelsey should have slept on the long flight over the Atlantic, especially because he had barely slept the last few days, instead preferring to stare into space and replay the awful event in his mind. Would it have turned out differently if his head had been in the game? If he had been paying better attention instead of focusing on pot roast, would Lolly still be alive?

He always came back to the same answer: no. Even if he had been thinking about pot roast, his head *had* been in the game. He had been aware and alert. His spidey senses had tingled, alerting him to the danger. It was why they had moved in close, shielding Shelby as they formed a circle around her. It was that circle that had not only saved her but himself, Nick, and Truck. If they hadn't had that prescient warning that something was about to happen, then they would all be dead.

There was nothing that would have saved Lolly unless maybe the pickup hadn't been changed. Kelsey could waste time being angry at the higher ups, but what was the point? His anger wouldn't change anything. They would never learn from their mistakes; they would continue to mess with the lives of men on the ground because that was what they did.

His anger was useless, his grief hadn't hit yet, so where did that leave him? Dreading, that's where. Undoubtedly Melly had been told the news. He knew because Nick had called her. Truck had called her. He should have called her, but he couldn't. She was going to fall apart; she was going to need comfort, and he couldn't deal with the fallout from across the ocean. He needed to see her, to hold her, to try and piece her back together in person.

He thought he was the only one in a reclining position, staring at the airplane ceiling, but then Truck spoke. "You guys awake?"

"Yeah," Nick said.

"Me, too," Kelsey replied.

They were silent a few more minutes, commiserating in silent grief. "I don't know how I'm going to handle Melly," Kelsey said at last.

"What do you mean handle her?" Truck asked. "She's crying, you hold her. That's it."

"I've never seen her cry before," Kelsey said. "I don't think I'm up for this."

"You swore to do it," Truck said, which was a really cruddy thing to say at the moment. As if Kelsey wasn't freaking out enough. How was he supposed to take care of Melly? He could barely take care of himself.

"Truck's right, Kelse," Nick added. "You put your arms around her and hold her. Be a strong shoulder for her to lean on. That's all she wants right now, someone to hold her through her grief. Besides, she's been staying with Ash and the family since it happened. She's not totally alone, and she's coping. Ashleigh said she's been holding up pretty well."

Kelsey shook his head. "That's because they don't have the kind of bond we do. She's going to lose it when she sees me, just totally fall apart."

"Don't be afraid," Truck said. The words bore his usual no-holds-barred delivery, but they were laced with a new tenderness Kelsey found disconcerting. Too much was changing—Truck wasn't allowed to change, too. "Opening yourself up and letting someone in isn't so bad."

Kelsey rolled his eyes, but the cabin was so dark the action was covered. *Thank you, Oprah,* he refrained from saying, but barely. Truck didn't understand, no one understood. He simply wasn't equipped to be a caregiver. Some men were cut out for it, he wasn't. And now he was going to have to walk Melly through what was undoubtedly the worst thing that would ever happen to her. How was he going to do it?

He worried over the problem all the way to the US and on the smaller jet to their base in North Carolina. Then the time for thinking was over. A long line of marines stood at attention as the plane landed and their team disembarked. Kelsey, Nick, and Truck took their place at the end of the line. Truck was in his wheelchair, but he saluted. They all did as Lolly's flag-draped coffin was unloaded and rolled slowly through the long line of marines. Nick was crying again, and Ashton was too. Kelsey had never seen Ashton cry before this mission. He didn't want to see it again. Why couldn't people suck it up and keep it together?

They followed the coffin into the building where Ashleigh, Caleigh, their parents and Melly were waiting. Melly was biting her lip, standing on her toes to see over the crowd, looking for him. She saw him and sank back onto her heels, still biting her lip as she searched his face. He did the same to her and noted that she was dry-eyed. That was all going to change as soon as he reached her. He could see it, could see her barely containing her emotion.

He stopped short in front of her. "Melly, I..." and then the unexpected happened. Melly remained tearless while he lost it completely. It was as if he wasn't even in control of his body anymore as wave after wave of sobs overtook him. His head dropped to his hands, and Melly was there, gathering him close against her chest, soothing him like a mother soothes a baby.

"It's all right, Kelsey. It's going to be all right."

But Kelsey knew she was lying because it would never be all right again.

. . .

THANK YOU FOR READING *GUNNER*, the second Brothers Courageous book. The story continues in book three, Spotter. For more books, please check out my website www.vanessagraybartal.com

9 781953 339072